He flicked over to the photograph he'd taken of her in the library.

"*This* is you," he said, his voice cracking. "The you I saw. The you I kissed on the beach. The you I wanted to kiss among the bluebells this morning, when you were pretending to be me and bossing me about." He paused. "The you I want to kiss now, even though I know it's unfair of me because you have to go back to San Rocello and you have duties to fulfill. The you I want to kiss now, even though I'm not looking for a relationship—and even if I was, I know there isn't a snowflake's chance in hell of things working out between us."

She knew he was right.

She could be sensible Princess Vittoria, agree with him there wasn't a hope for them and walk away.

Or she could be herself. The woman who wanted him to kiss her. Who wanted to kiss him back. Who wanted more.

Just for tonight...

Dear Reader,

Have you ever wanted to take some time out, just for you? But how much harder would it be if you're constantly in the public eye? I've always loved the film *Roman Holiday*, but life is so different now that the princess's escape could never work. I thought about it...and that's when I came up with the idea of *Surprise Heir for the Princess*. And who better to help her escape than someone who really understands the media—a photographer!

So Liam helps Vittoria be not-a-princess for a few days. He takes her to a little cottage by the sea (yes, of course, in my own favorite place in Norfolk) and helps her find who the woman behind the tiara really is. Neither of them plans to fall in love with the other...but one night of talking really truthfully under the stars leads to an unexpected complication.

Can they find their way between duty and ambition toward true love? You'll have to read on to find out!

With love,

Kate Hardy

Surprise Heir for the Princess

—

Kate Hardy

HARLEQUIN®

Romance™

Recycling programs
for this product may
not exist in your area.

ISBN-13: 978-1-335-56696-6

Surprise Heir for the Princess

Copyright © 2021 by Pamela Brooks

This edition published by arrangement with Harlequin Books S.A.

For questions and comments about the quality of this book,
please contact us at CustomerService@Harlequin.com.

Harlequin Enterprises ULC
22 Adelaide St. West, 40th Floor
Toronto, Ontario M5H 4E3, Canada
www.Harlequin.com

Printed in U.S.A.

Kate Hardy has been a bookworm since she was a toddler. When she isn't writing, Kate enjoys reading, theater, live music, ballet and the gym. She lives with her husband, student children and their spaniel in Norwich, England. You can contact her via her website: katehardy.com.

Books by Kate Hardy

Harlequin Romance

A Crown by Christmas

Soldier Prince's Secret Baby Gift

Summer at Villa Rosa

The Runaway Bride and the Billionaire

Christmas Bride for the Boss
Reunited at the Altar
A Diamond in the Snow
Finding Mr. Right in Florence
One Night to Remember
A Will, a Wish, a Wedding

Harlequin Medical Romance

Changing Shifts

Fling with Her Hot-Shot Consultant

A Nurse and a Pup to Heal Him
Mistletoe Proposal on the Children's Ward
Forever Family for the Midwife

Visit the Author Profile page
at Harlequin.com for more titles.

For Gerard, with all my love

Praise for
Kate Hardy

CHAPTER ONE

THE VIEW FROM the ferry was almost enough to persuade Liam to give up portraits for landscape photography. A milky turquoise sea reflecting the deep red ball of the setting sun, a sky that looked almost airbrushed from hazy blue at the horizon to deep peach at the top, and the sun itself starting to dip behind the silhouetted island of San Rocello. He'd never seen anything so gorgeous.

But he wasn't here on holiday; he was here to take the official photographs of Princess Vittoria di Sarda, before her grandfather stepped down and she took over as the ruler of the little Mediterranean kingdom.

Although Liam's discussions with the king's private secretary had gone some way to reassuring him that he'd been chosen on the merit of his work, the commission still felt a bit like nepotism. The princess's younger sister Isabella happened to be his own little sister Saoirse's best friend, and he knew that Izzy had suggested him to her grandfather for the job.

He took a deep breath. This flutter of nerves was absolutely ridiculous. He'd photographed plenty of people for upmarket magazines and Sunday supplements, including A-list celebrities and high-ranking politicians. Some of his work hung in the National Portrait Gallery in London. And he'd honed his social skills during his apprenticeship, so he was comfortable mixing at any level of society.

But this was the first time he'd been commissioned to take a royal portrait.

And he had a fine line to walk. The private secretary had explained that the king wanted a formal portrait of the future queen. Izzy had scoffed. 'Nonno will want you to take something stuffy, with Rina dolled up in a posh frock, dripping in jewels and wearing a sash.'

'That's pretty standard stuff for a princess,' Liam had pointed out.

'And it's about a century out of date,' Izzy had grumbled. 'I hate the way the palace stifles her. The world needs to see the woman behind the tiara.'

The woman behind the tiara.

All the press photographs and the paparazzi snaps Liam had seen of Vittoria di Sarda showed a cool, collected and businesslike woman. Perfectly groomed, always with a faint smile. Not quite Mona Lisa, but heading that way. She certainly wasn't a scatty ball of energy, like her little sister; looking at Izzy, seeing her laugh in his kitchen with his sister and munching toast, anyone would think that she was just another art student rather than a princess. Vittoria, on the other hand, looked every inch a royal.

The portrait her grandfather wanted would work perfectly well. Vittoria traditionally wore her dark hair in a classic and slightly old-fashioned style that reminded Liam of Grace Kelly; she had a gorgeous bone structure, and arresting violet eyes that reminded him of a young Elizabeth Taylor. She could definitely carry off the traditional pose with posh frock, diamonds and royal regalia.

But Izzy had also shown him some selfies from her phone, just to prove her own description. 'See? She looks like sunshine when she smiles.'

Vittoria di Sarda looked much softer in those candid snaps. Sweeter. She glowed. She didn't look like the woman who was about to start running a country; she looked approachable and warm.

He shook himself.

He shouldn't be thinking along those lines.

Apart from the fact that he'd never get involved with a client, he'd learned the hard way that careers and relationships didn't mix. He'd already done the raising a family bit, when he was eighteen and Saoirse was twelve; although he'd never regretted his decision to walk away from his place at university to get a job and look after his little sister, ensuring she wasn't taken into care, his girlfriends had resented the time he'd spent with his sister. Some of them had taken the 'it's not you, it's me' tack when they'd dumped him, but the more honest ones had said they didn't want to settle down and raise a young teenager when they weren't much older than that themselves. They'd wanted to go out to parties and have fun, not stay at home. The fact that Saoirse was his only living relative and really important to him had just passed them by.

Later on, when Saoirse was older and didn't need him so much, his girlfriends had resented the time he spent on his career. Time spent travelling, or on a shoot, or in his darkroom, or working on a digital image. They couldn't see the tiny differences on an image that he could, and got fed up hanging around waiting for him.

Liam was tired of being torn in two and made to feel guilty, so he'd kept all his relationships casual over the last few years. He wanted to focus on his career, on his goal: of becoming the best portrait photographer of his generation.

And maybe, just maybe, Vittoria di Sarda would be the one to help him get there.

Vittoria finished reading her dossier.

Liam MacCarthy, photographer and older brother of her little sister Izzy's best friend. A man who'd turned down a place at university after their mother had been killed, who'd brought up his sister and who still lived with her in London. A nice guy, according to both Izzy and Pietro, Izzy's bodyguard; it seemed he'd taken Izzy under his wing, too, over the last three years. A man whose actions showed he believed in family and duty, just like hers.

But this commission to take her official portrait wasn't nepotism. He was good at his job. Seriously good. His work featured in up-market magazines and Sunday supplements, and he already had work hanging in the National Portrait Gallery in London. He'd take the kind of portrait her grandfather wanted, and do it well.

Even so, Vittoria wasn't looking forward to the sitting. Over the last year, she'd felt more and more stifled at the palace. She was prepared to become queen—since her father's untimely death in a yachting accident when she was eleven, she'd been pretty much in training to step up to the throne—but her mother and grandmother were pressuring her to make a dynastic marriage before her coronation.

Once, she'd dreamed of marrying for love. Rufus, the fellow student she'd fallen head over heels for during their MBA year, seemed to feel the same way about her; and he'd loved her for herself, not because she was Princess Vittoria di Sarda of San Rocello. She'd thought he was going to ask her to marry him. Until he'd actually met her family and realised that their life together would be lived on the equivalent of a floodlit stage; Rufus had backed away, saying that he loved her, but he really couldn't handle the royal lifestyle.

It had taught Vittoria that love wasn't compatible with duty. But she still couldn't quite bring herself to agree to get engaged to José, the son of a Spanish duke that her mother and grandmother had lined up as an eligible suitor. They'd met a few times socially and had absolutely nothing in common. But time—and suitable men—were both running out. She had to make a decision. Sooner, rather than later, with her grandfather wanting to step down at the end of the year.

If only she could escape for a few days to

clear her head. Somewhere she could think
things through without any pressure...

The next morning, Liam headed for the Pala-
zzo Reale in the centre of the capital. The
palace was a huge Renaissance-era building,
built from pale cream stone; its tall windows
were flanked with louvred shutters, painted
the same cream as the stone. The imposing
entrance had marble steps leading up to huge
bronze doors.

Liam re-read the instructions in the email
from the Private Secretary, Matteo Battaglia; he went over to the security checkpoint
to introduce himself, then went through the
security procedure before being escorted to
the Private Secretary's office by one of the
guards.

'Delighted to meet you, Mr MacCarthy.' The
Private Secretary shook his hand.

'*Buongiorno*. Delighted to meet you, too,
Signor Battaglia,' Liam responded.

Signor Battiglia gave him an approving
smile and took him through to the king's office.

Liam remembered what Izzy had told him
when he'd asked how he should address her
family. It was the same as for the English royal
family; he should call her grandfather 'Your

Majesty' and Vittoria 'Your Royal Highness' the first time, and then 'sir' or 'ma'am'.

He waited politely for the king to speak.

'Good morning, Mr MacCarthy.' King Vittorio held out his hand for Liam to shake.

'*Buongiorno, Vostro Maestà.* Thank you for inviting me here.'

The royal visage was completely impassive and Liam didn't have a clue what was going through the king's head. 'Princess Isabella speaks highly of you.'

'That's good to know, sir.' All this formality made the neck of Liam's shirt feel tight; Liam rarely wore a suit at work, but today was definitely a suit and tie day. What he really wanted to do was to get his camera out and start work.

There was a slight twinkle in King Vittorio's eye when he added, 'Though Izzy also says your coffee is atrocious.'

It broke the ice and Liam laughed, relaxing for the first time since he'd walked into the palace. 'I'm afraid my barista skills aren't quite up to my darkroom skills, sir.'

'So you'll be using traditional film rather than digital?'

Liam was pleased that the king was aware of the difference. 'A mixture, sir,' he said. 'I use a digital camera a lot of the time, but I like analogue. There's something special about developing a print.'

'Indeed.' King Vittorio inclined his head. 'I liked the photographs you took for that article on Shakespearean actors. Quite remarkable how you dressed them all in plain black and yet they still looked like the characters of their most famous roles.'

And that was enough to finally convince Liam that he'd been given the job on merit and not just because of his little sister's friendship with Izzy. The king had actually seen his work and liked it. 'Thank you, sir. I asked them to declaim their favourite speeches and took the shots as they talked. I think a face should always tell the story in a portrait.'

The king made a noncommittal noise. 'Let's take you to Vittoria. She's waiting for us in the Throne Room. Walk with me,' he added imperiously.

Didn't protocol mean that you had to walk behind a king? Liam wondered. But the king had said to walk *with* him. Perhaps he could compromise by being half a step behind.

Liam hauled his tripod and camera over his shoulder and walked through the corridor with the king. The place was amazing and, although he specialised in portraits, there were plenty of little details that made him itch to photograph them. The black and white marble floors, the full-length windows hung with voile curtains, the silk wall hangings. And he'd just bet there was a suite of rooms with a classic enfilade, where the doors between each room were so perfectly aligned that you could see every doorway from one end of the suite. He could just imagine taking a series of portraits of the princess, one in every doorway...

Then they walked into the Throne Room. The red carpet was so thick that Liam literally sank into it with every step. The walls were hung with red damask silk; the high ceilings were painted in cream and gold, and Venetian gilt and glass chandeliers hung down, glittering. On one wall there was an oil painting of King Vittorio, next to portraits of various others that Liam assumed were former kings; all were set in heavy, ornate gold frames. There was a white marble fireplace with a mirror above it reflecting the chandeliers, and on the mantelshelf sat an ornate ormolu clock flanked by matching candelabra.

It was all very traditional, and a portrait taken here would send out a very strong message.

There were two thrones in red velvet on a raised dais at the far end of the room. Sitting on one of the thrones, reading, was a young woman.

Vittoria di Sarda.

'Vittoria, may I introduce Liam MacCarthy, photographer? Mr MacCarthy, this is my granddaughter, Princess Vittoria,' King Vittorio said.

She closed her book, setting it down on the throne next to her, and stood up.

The press photographs and even Izzy's snaps hadn't done her any justice.

Vittoria di Sarda was absolutely stunning.

You could drown in the depths of those violet eyes.

Liam opened his mouth and found himself silenced. Not good. He wanted her to see him as he was: a professional, not some tongue-tied bumbler.

He'd met lots of beautiful women in his working life, and dated several equally beautiful women in his private life, but none of them had made his pulse race like this.

'I'm delighted to meet you, *Vostra Altezza Reale*,' he said, just about managing to string the words together. Thank God Izzy and her bodyguard Pietro had spent the last week schooling his Italian pronunciation and teaching him important phrases. Otherwise he might have accidentally called her a festering slug or something equally terrible instead of 'Your Royal Highness'.

'My sister's said a lot about you, Mr Mac-Carthy,' she said, offering him her hand to shake.

His skin tingled where hers touched his, and he didn't know what to say.

This was crazy. He wasn't a talker, as such, but he was always good with his clients, conversing just enough to put them at their ease. If he carried on like this, the portrait he ended up with would be even worse than the stuffy waxwork Izzy was worried he might end up taking.

He dragged himself together with an effort. 'Thank you for sparing the time to see me, ma'am.'

'You could hardly take my portrait without me actually being here,' she pointed out.

Was she teasing him or irritated by him? He couldn't tell. That beautiful face was inscrutable.

Best to play it safe and be businesslike. 'With your permission, ma'am, I'll set up my equipment.' At her nod, he did so in silence, but he kept glancing at her. She was dressed perfectly for the formal, old-fashioned portrait that Vittorio had requested, in a white haute couture gown teamed with a midnight-blue velvet cloak, a sash and a royal badge. Her hair was styled very simply, and she wore a tiara with matching earrings, necklace and bracelet.

Dripping in diamonds.

Was that what people wanted from a modern princess? Wealth, haughtiness and an air of distance? Or did they want something warmer, a view of a woman who had something in common with them?

Liam itched to take a different set of photographs from the one he'd been commissioned to do. To remove the sash and the diamonds, replace them with single pearl earrings and a single-strand pearl necklace, and end up with a softer and sexier look—like Beaton's 1954 portrait of Elizabeth Taylor or Karsh's gorgeous 1956 portrait of Grace Kelly.

Maybe he could talk her into letting him take a second set of portraits. Especially as he'd promised to take one for Izzy.

Though he wanted to take one for himself, too. He wanted to see the woman behind the tiara. The woman she kept hidden. The woman whose smile was like sunshine.

'I'll leave you to it,' King Vittorio said.

'Thank you, sir.'

'Give my love to my granddaughter when you're back in London.'

'Of course, sir.'

Liam waited until the king had left. Vittoria, while she was waiting for him to finish setting up, had her nose back in her book. He couldn't resist a quick snap.

The sound of the shutter alerted her, and she stared at him. 'Why did you do that?'

'Testing for white balance, ma'am,' he fibbed.

'I won't insult you, Mr MacCarthy, by saying that I hope none of the photographs you take today appear anywhere without the prior approval of the palace press office,' she said coolly.

She really *was* a royal, he thought. An ice princess. But he'd like to see more of the woman he thought she might be behind that image. The sister Izzy had described—the woman who'd been sitting lost in a book. That moment had reminded him of his sister, when she was small: how Saoirse had always lost herself in a book, like her favourite fairy tale princess Belle.

Was that who Vittoria was, behind the tiara?

'Of course, ma'am.' Wanting to reassure her, he added, 'The contract I signed stipulated that all negatives and original files will be the property of the House of di Sarda, to use as you wish, and I'll be credited with the images.'

'Good. Then let's get this over with.'

Interesting, he thought. As a woman who was destined to be a queen, she must surely have grown up very used to having her photograph taken. He couldn't help wondering: did she, like Izzy, want a different portrait from the one her grandfather had commissioned?

He looked at her. 'Once we've taken the official portraits, ma'am, would you allow me to take a portrait for Izzy? I mean, Princess Isabella,' he corrected himself swiftly. He didn't have the same easy, familiar relationship with this woman that he did with her sister, so he needed to be more formal in the way he referred to Izzy.

She tipped her head very slightly to one side, and his pulse went up another notch as he realised how beautiful her mouth was. *Kissable*. He really had to get a grip.

'What does Izzy want?' Princess Vittoria asked, surprising him with a lapse into informality.

He was taking a risk, but he caught her fleeting expression and it gave him the courage to be honest. 'Something that makes you—and I quote—not look like a stuffed waxwork.'

She laughed, and for the first time he saw a glimpse of the sister Izzy adored. At that moment he knew that *this* was the woman he wanted to photograph, not the official Princess.

'That sounds like Izzy.' She paused. 'Your little sister's best friend.'

He inclined his head. 'I'm sure your security

team has a dossier on me.' What did surprise
him was that she might have bothered to read
it.

She inclined her head. 'Let me see. Aged
thirty. Never married. Didn't go to university—
but you finished your A levels while looking
after your sister, and then you took an apprenticeship.'

He shrugged. 'University wasn't an option. It's irrelevant.' But he knew just as much
about her, thanks to some research on the
internet and a conversation or two with her
sister. 'Did you enjoy studying in London—
economics for your first degree and then for
your MBA?'

Toccato,' she said. 'You clearly have a dossier on me.'

'I need to know my subjects before I take
their portrait,' he said. 'The whole point of a
portrait is to tell a story. To show the world
who you really are.'

'Goodness. That's frightfully intimidating.'

He threw the ball back in her court. 'Only
if you have something to hide.'

'Call me Dorianna Grey?'

There was an edge to her humour.

He couldn't work her out. They'd never met
before. And yet the way he found himself instinctively responding to her... *My dear Lady*

Disdain. Except Vittoria was a few rungs higher up the social scale than a lady.

He looked into those stunning violet eyes and, for a second, he couldn't breathe. And then, shockingly, he realised how much he wanted to kiss her. To feel her mouth against his. To coax a response from her. To kiss her until they were both dizzy.

That desire was completely inappropriate, for a multitude of reasons. Vittoria di Sarda was his client, and he never mixed business with pleasure. She was the sister of his little sister's best friend, which made her pretty much off limits; because when it got messy—and it *would* get messy—that would make life difficult for Saoirse. And Vittoria was from a completely different world, one where he didn't belong.

Focus, he reminded himself.

This was business.

'Izzy loves you,' he said.

'And Saoirse loves you.'

He liked the fact that she pronounced his sister's name properly. *Sur-sha.* 'She's a good kid.'

Vittoria raised an eyebrow. 'You could have gone to university.'

Not to Edinburgh, where he'd planned to study. They'd lost their mum five months before his A levels, in a car accident; how could he uproot Saoirse and drag her off to a city where she knew nobody and where he'd be too busy studying to spend enough time with her to help her settle in properly? Becoming a teenager was hard enough; he'd wanted to keep things as stable for her as he could, which meant she needed to stay at the home and school she knew. 'I have a diploma and plenty of professional experience. A degree wouldn't have added anything.'

'You put your duty before your own needs,' she said softly.

His duty to look after Saoirse. There hadn't been anyone else to do it; their father had died when Saoirse was small and their grandparents had either been very elderly and needing care themselves or had passed away.

But it hadn't just been duty, and he wanted Vittoria to know that. He'd never seen Saoirse as a burden and he never would. 'My sister isn't my duty,' he said, equally softly. 'She's my *family*.'

Again, there was a fleeting expression in her eyes before the royal mask came back. But it was there for long enough for him to see it and recognise it as wistfulness.

So was Izzy right? Was Vittoria suppressing herself for the sake of duty? Because she loved her family?

Not that it was any of his business.

'What else is in your dossier?' she asked.

'That you're a patron of several charities.' Izzy hadn't been clear about whether Vittoria had chosen them herself or whether their grandfather had chosen them.

And then there was the duty aspect. 'That you lost your dad when you were young—' like him '—so you're next in line to the throne and your coronation will be at Christmas,' he added.

'Nonno wishes to stand down,' she said.

'And how do you feel, becoming the Queen of San Rocello at the age of twenty-eight?'

'That,' she said, 'is irrelevant.'

Echoing his own answer to her. And that told him everything: like him, she'd chosen duty before her own desires. And she'd made that choice for the love of her family.

Though he did need to know how she felt. It would affect the portrait.

Maybe he could try a different tack. But what?

Not her love life. Although the paparazzi had photographed her with several eligible men over the years, she didn't appear to have a partner. Though Izzy had muttered something dark about their mother, their grandmother and an arranged marriage.

Could someone royal marry for love? Or did they have to marry someone politically suitable?

Not that *that* was any of his business, either.

'What were you reading?' he asked instead.

She raised an eyebrow. 'What do you think I was reading?'

This felt like a test. Fiction, non-fiction, poetry, a play? He had no idea what she liked reading, but he definitely had the impression that words were important to her. 'If you were Izzy, it'd be something frothy. If you were Saoirse, it'd be something political. If you were me...' He looked her straight in the eye. 'Words, words, words,' he quoted softly.

She laughed. 'So which of us is Polonius?'

He was pleased she'd picked up the reference. 'Neither, I hope. Though he did have a point about being true to yourself.'

'Is that why you take portraits?'

'People interest me,' he said.

'And you read Shakespeare? Or was *Hamlet* your A level text?'

'The dossier again?' he asked.

'Photography, English Literature, History and History of Art.' She ticked off his subjects on her fingers.

'Economics, Maths and History,' he countered. Subjects perfect for a future queen: a background in tradition, with modern business sensibilities. 'Mine were pretty much your opposite, though obviously there's a bit of science in photography—physics and chemistry.'

Chemistry.

That was a stupid word to use. Because it made him think of a different sort of chemistry. The one that made him notice the exact curve of her mouth, the length of her eyelashes, the tilt of her nose.

Focus, he reminded himself again. 'Would you prefer your official photographer to have a degree?'

'No. I was wondering if you minded. Four top-grade A levels—you could've had your pick of any university.'

He'd be honest with her. 'I minded a bit when I was eighteen,' he said. 'But Saoirse was more important to me. Twelve isn't a great age to move to a different school, let alone a different city. I still ended up with the career I wanted; the apprenticeship meant I learned my trade hands-on instead of in a lecture room. And my old photography tutor lent me books and invited Saoirse and me over for dinner once a month so I could talk theory with her and discuss composition, while Saoirse did the usual teenage girl things with her daughters. I owe her a lot.'

'The woman you dedicated your first award to.'

He nodded. And not just because of the tuition. Patty had helped him convince the authorities that he was perfectly capable of looking after Saoirse. Luckily his mum had already taught him how to cook a few simple dishes, so he'd be able to look after himself as a student. His mum had owned the house outright since his dad's death; and the proceeds of her life insurance meant that he and Saoirse could pay the bills until he was earning a decent salary and could support them both. 'And if she could see me now, she'd be cross that I was chatting about myself instead of focusing on my subject.'

'Very diplomatically put,' she said. 'I can see why Izzy likes you.'

'I like Izzy. And she's safe with me.'

'I already knew that,' she said.

'Because of the dossier?'

'Because Pietro likes you,' she corrected.

She'd discussed him with her sister's security detail?

And then he realised. This was what her life must be like. A series of dossiers, learning about people so you could be politically discreet. Knowing that everything you did, everything you said, would be analysed, and not always correctly. Living your life in the public eye, twenty-four-seven.

Which was exactly why King Vittorio had asked for a traditional portrait, Liam realised. To put across the message that the public face of the monarchy might change, but the monarchy itself would go on.

Why hadn't Izzy told her that Liam MacCarthy was gorgeous?

Tall, with dark hair he'd clearly tried to tame today in deference to his royal clients, cornflower-blue eyes and fair skin. And the most beautiful mouth…

She shook herself. Ridiculous. Liam MacCarthy was here to take her portrait, that was all.

Nothing could possibly happen between them. They were from different worlds and she'd learned from Rufus that getting involved with someone not from her own background led to heartbreak.

She ought to just let him get on with this. Let him take the portrait her grandfather wanted, then leave.

But he was the first man in years who'd made her feel a spark. Who'd fenced with her, responded to teasing.

She'd liked his quick wit. The way he'd quoted Shakespeare at her and picked up her veiled references—unlike José, who'd simply looked blank and turned the conversation back to cars.

Liam MacCarthy intrigued her.

Which was exactly why she should be on her utmost regal dignity with him. She couldn't afford to react to him as a man.

'Where do you want me?' The words slipped out before she could stop them.

Oh, no. That sounded like flirting. 'To sit for the portrait, I mean,' she added swiftly. 'Unless you'd prefer me to stand.'

He gave her an assessing look, and heat curled up through her, from the bottom of her feet to the top of her head. 'If you don't mind, ma'am, I'd like to take a range of shots.'

Back to the formal 'ma'am'.

Of course he wouldn't call her Rina, the way her sister did—short for Vittorina, her family pet name. He wouldn't even call her Vittoria. To him, she was Your Royal Highness or ma'am.

Sometimes, protocol really grated on her; yet, at the same time as it made her feel boxed in, she recognised that it protected her.

He directed her to sit, to stand, to change position. He changed the lighting and worked almost in silence. Vittoria felt herself growing more and more twitchy, then her impatience finally burst out. 'Do all your sittings take this long?'

'That depends, ma'am, on my subject.'

She met his gaze; he masked it quickly, but for a moment she was sure she could see the same heat in his eyes that she felt pulsing through her.

'The sitting goes more quickly for both of us if my subject talks to me,' he said. 'Like the ones I did of the Shakespearean actors. They declaimed their favourite speeches from their favourite roles.'

Sometimes it felt as if she were playing a role. But she didn't have any new speeches. 'So is this where I tell you all about San Rocello, its exports and its history?'

'You could—but that's the economist in you talking.' He paused. 'Tell me what you love doing. Tell me about your passion.'

Passion. Something else she had to suppress. A queen couldn't be passionate. A queen needed to be diplomatic and sensible. A royal first and a woman second.

Looking at his mouth, she could imagine it moving in passion, and she had to suppress the sudden shiver of desire.

Things weren't meant to be this way, and it tipped her off balance. It also made her cross with herself. She'd been trained to react with dignity and calm. A queen-in-waiting. But something about him made her react to him as a woman—something deep and primeval and which she didn't really understand. She wasn't sure whether it scared her more or excited her.

What did she say?

She glanced round the room.

Thankfully someone had put a silver bowl of roses on a low table and she seized on them gratefully. 'Roses,' she said. 'They're my passion.'

'Sadly, it's slightly too early in the year for roses, or I'd suggest a few shots by the roses I assume are in the palace gardens,' he said. 'But you can tell me about your favourite rose. Describe its colour, its scent, the touch of its petals.'

His voice was husky and incredibly sensual, and her mind was translating his words into something else entirely.

Please don't let the heat she could feel in her cheeks actually be visible.

'Ma'am?'

'Call me Vittoria.' The words came out before she could stop them.

'Vittoria,' he said softly.

And, oh, she could imagine him saying that as he drew her into his arms for a kiss…

She shook herself. 'I was lying about the roses.'

'Would I be right in guessing books are your passion?'

Yes, and she didn't get anywhere near enough time to read. Which made her feel even more trapped and frustrated—but she didn't want him to guess that. It was private. Something she needed to keep to herself. She shrugged. 'You saw me reading when you came here.'

'And the palace has a library?'

'Yes, of course.'

'Show me, Vittoria.'

It wasn't so much a command as a request. A temptation. She didn't dare move.

'When Saoirse was small,' he said, 'her favourite story was *Beauty and the Beast*. She loved the film, too, and she used to sing the soundtrack all the time. Mum and I took her to see the stage show for her birthday when she was seven. I remember, it was a matinee. Not the sort of thing your average thirteen-year-old boy would put up with, but I went because I knew it'd make my mum and my sister happy. She loved every second, and she loved it even more when we went for dinner afterwards and the waitress lowered the lights and came out carrying an ice-cream with a fountain candle.

The whole restaurant sang "Happy Birthday" to her.'

The yearning in his eyes as he shared the memory made Vittoria's heart crack a little.

'That was a bright spot. And I used to tease her that she should have been called Belle.' His eyes met hers. 'And I have a feeling that might be who you really are. The princess who loves stories. The princess whose dream is a castle filled with books.'

He was the first person she'd ever met who'd seen that.

So, instead of ignoring his request, she nodded and beckoned to him to follow her.

CHAPTER TWO

THE SECOND THEY were in the palace library, Liam's face lit up. 'What a fabulous room. This is perfect. This is where I want to take a photograph of you for Izzy. But you'll need to lose the diamonds.'

'Lose the diamonds?'

He sighed. 'All right. I'll take one with the diamonds, for your grandfather. But do you have a maid or something who can bring you pearls instead?'

'Pearls?' And now Vittoria knew she sounded stupid. As if she were parroting his words.

He took his phone from his pocket and drew up a photograph. 'Like this,' he said.

The subject of the portrait was instantly recognisable. 'Princess Grace of Monaco.'

'It's by Yousuf Karsh. One of the two photographers whose work I admire the most,' he said. 'The simplicity means people focus on the subject, not the trapping. And what I want is you without the diamonds, with a book in your hand, sitting on that window seat. Then I want you to read me your favourite poem.'

No more 'ma'am', she thought. He'd forgotten the protocol completely, to the point where he was bossing her about and telling her what to do. But this was Liam MacCarthy all fired up, seeing a vision he wanted to capture behind his lens. Was this what drove him? She found his purpose and focus irresistible.

'Take the portrait for Nonno, first,' she said, 'while someone fetches the jewellery you want me to wear.' She went to have a quiet word with the footman who waited at the doorway, then followed Liam's directions and posed for a portrait that he deemed suitable for her grandfather.

There was a discreet cough and the footman placed the jewels Liam had asked for on a low table.

'Thank you,' she said. In her view, the staff weren't the invisible servants they might have been a hundred years before. She'd been brought up knowing that their staff did their job so she could do hers, and without them life would be a lot less smooth. They deserved her respect as well as their salary.

'That's perfect. *Grazie,*' Liam added.

She liked the fact that he'd thanked her staff, and she liked it even more that he'd bothered to do it in their own language. This was a man who didn't take things for granted, then. She knew from the dossier that his flat in Chelsea was worth a lot of money, but she now also knew he'd worked for it.

'Do you need help with your jewellery, ma'am?' he asked.

She raised an eyebrow. 'This is the twenty-first century, not two hundred years ago. Princesses are perfectly capable of dressing themselves.'

Amusement glittered in those gorgeous eyes. 'To be fair, two hundred years ago, with all those tiny buttons down the back of a dress, princesses would've needed someone to help them.'

'And how would you know about…? Oh.' It dawned on her. 'You did a photo shoot.'

He inclined his head. 'Plus, Saoirse did a module on the history of fashion, and part of the assessment included being involved in an exhibition of Regency clothing at the V&A.'

Which obviously he'd taken an interest in, and probably attended. She liked that.

But the idea of him taking off her jewellery made her feel flustered. It was too intimate. 'I can manage,' she said, taking off the tiara and putting it on the table next to the pearls. Her earrings and necklace were next. She replaced them with the simple pearl studs and single string of pearls. And how ridiculous that her hands were shaking slightly. Why on earth was she imagining him lifting her hair away from her nape and pressing a kiss on the skin he uncovered, before fastening the pearls round her neck? Crazy. She *never* had thoughts like this, particularly about someone she'd only just met.

'Is this what you had in mind?' Worse still, her voice was slightly quavery. She really hoped he hadn't noticed.

He stepped back, narrowing his eyes, and assessed her.

She thought—hoped—it was a professional gaze.

'Take off the cloak, the sash and the badge,' he said.

Her dress would be more than acceptable at any society event; it was shoulderless, but perfectly demure. She'd be exposing far more skin if she wore a swimsuit. So why did it make her feel as if she was undressing for him when she took off the cloak, sash and badge?

'And your shoes,' he said. 'I'd like you to sit on the window seat. Draw your feet up and look out of the window.'

She did so. Despite the fact there was a footman in the room with them—and if anyone walked in, they'd simply see a photographer working with his subject—this felt incredibly intimate. As if they were alone. Nobody but the

two of them in the whole world. Everyone and
everything else just dropped away; she was
only aware of Liam. His nearness. The way
he looked at her. His mouth. His breathing.

And it was the first time in so long that she'd
felt *herself* at the palace. Unfettered. Unstifled.
Just Vittoria.

She'd already worked out that, as a portrait
photographer, Liam tended to see a little more
deeply and pick up more cues than the average person. Would he see that this was the real
her, not the princess? And, if so, what would
he do about it?

'One more prop,' he said, and took a book
from the nearest shelf.

It was a slim volume in red Morocco bind-
ing, tooled with gold.

And how incredible that he'd chosen a book
at random that she would have picked, given
the choice: a copy of Shakespeare's sonnets.

Liam asked her to change position on the
window seat several more times, then frowned.
'No. I know what's wrong.' He stepped forward. 'May I?'

She didn't have a clue what he intended, but
now he was really up close and personal. His
eyes were stunning, and his pupils were so
huge that she couldn't see his irises. Was that
because of the lower level of light in the room?

Or did he feel that same crazy attraction that made her pulse skip?

He stretched one hand towards her and she held her breath for a second.

He mussed her hair slightly; his fingers accidentally brushed her skin and made her feel as if she were burning.

She could feel her lips parting. Could see the expression in his eyes change as he looked at her mouth. Could see his own lips parting.

For a heartbeat, everything stopped; it felt as if it was just the two of them, the sunlight filtering through the window and dancing across their skin. It would be so easy to cross that tiny distance between them. All she had to do was stretch up, very slightly, and kiss him…

Then he coughed and stepped away. 'Ma'am.'

Vittoria felt the colour rush into her cheeks, along with shame. For pity's sake. Liam Mac-Carthy was here to do a job, and that was all. She'd probably never see him again. He wasn't a man she should let herself moon over, particularly as she wasn't in a position to let herself moon over anyone.

'Read to me,' he said, his voice husky, and a frisson went down her spine.

Shakespeare's sonnets. She didn't need to open the book, because she knew her favourite one by heart; but she hoped that holding the book would act as enough of a barrier—so he'd see her as a queen-to-be, not the girl who dreamed of reading in a castle full of books. Because she knew Liam MacCarthy wasn't the Prince who'd build her a library and she had to put her duty first.

"'My mistress' eyes are nothing like the sun…'"

The beauty of the poem took over and she lost herself in the words, gazing out of the window.

She reached the bit that always amused her. "'I grant I never saw a goddess go; My mistress, when she walks, treads on the ground.'"

And then a soft, husky voice took up the final couplet: "'And yet, by heaven, I think my love as rare As any she belied with false compare.'"

She hadn't noticed that he'd walked back to her, right up close. She found herself gazing at him, rapt. Those beautiful words, in that beautiful soft Irish accent, held her spellbound.

He reached towards her, and she knew he was going to brush the pad of his thumb along her lower lip. A prelude to a kiss. This time, he wouldn't hold back. This time…

The clock on the mantelpiece chimed the quarter hour, and he drew his hand back.

'Thank you, ma'am, for your patience and co-operation.'

* * *

How stupid was he?

Liam was aghast at how he'd nearly made a complete mess of this—you never, ever, crossed the line between a professional relationship and a personal one. Especially when your subject was the granddaughter of a king. A woman who was about to become the queen of her Mediterranean realm.

He started to pack up his camera gear in silence, not trusting his mouth to come out with the wrong words and *really* drop him in it.

'Good afternoon, Mr MacCarthy,' she said, and he hated the way that the gorgeous, soft, sunshiny woman he'd almost kissed had turned back so quickly into the dignified, starchy princess he'd first met. Izzy had said her sister was stifled by the palace, and he could see that for himself. There was a huge difference between the almost shy girl in the library and this formal, regal woman who was very much in control of herself.

'Ma'am,' he said, giving her a clumsy half-bow.

'Give my regards to Princess Isabella when you see her next.'

Then she swept out of the room, where the temperature felt as if it had just dropped twenty degrees. The footman lingered until Liam had finished packing up his camera gear, then escorted him back to Matteo Battaglia's office.

'I trust all went well, Mr MacCarthy?' Signor Battaglia asked.

'I think so,' Liam said. 'Obviously I need to do some post-production work on the digital files and develop the negatives, but I'll take digital copies of the prints and give you an encrypted link to a gallery on my website so King Vittorio can choose which ones he'd like me to make finished prints of, then I'll courier the negatives and final prints to you in a couple of days. You have my details if you need to get in touch in the meantime.'

'Of course. I'll look forward to hearing from you.'

Liam was pretty sure that he wasn't supposed to ask to say goodbye to the king or to Vittoria. What was the protocol? Meeting Vittoria di Sarda had driven way too much out of his head. 'Please thank His Majesty and Her Royal Highness for their co-operation,' he said instead, and shook the Private Secretary's hand.

Then he brooded all the way back to his hotel, where he collected his travel baggage, settled his bill and checked out. He brooded all the way on the ferry back to mainland Italy. He brooded all the way on the plane back to

England and then the train and the Tube back to Chelsea. Thankfully Saoirse was out somewhere, so he brooded all the way to his darkroom; and he especially brooded when he developed the negatives.

The shots in the Throne Room were good. But the ones he'd taken for Izzy... Well, that wasn't true. He hadn't taken most of them for her. He'd taken them for *himself*. And they were spectacular. The best pictures he'd ever taken in his life. That last one, when he hadn't been able to resist finishing the sonnet for Vittoria, and she'd looked all dazed and sweet, and he'd been right on the cusp of kissing her...

God, he was an idiot.

No way would a princess even have a fling with him, let alone anything else.

And that last picture wasn't going to be seen by anyone except himself.

He'd hung the 'processing—do not disturb' sign on the door of his darkroom, so Saoirse wouldn't disturb him when she came in. He had enough time to finish developing the negatives as well as doing the post-production work on the digital files. Focusing on the technical side of things meant his emotions were perfectly buried by the time he emerged.

He followed his nose—takeaway pizza, he

was sure—to find Saoirse, Izzy and Pietro in the kitchen.

'Hey, there.' Saoirse greeted him with a hug. 'Did you have a good trip?'

Not quite how he'd phrase it, but he didn't want her to worry. 'Fine. And thanks for leaving me to my darkroom whenever you got in.'

'Of course. I know better than to risk ruining undeveloped negatives or a pile of new photographic paper. You drilled into me years ago that even a couple of seconds of light from the screen of a mobile phone would wreck things.' She smiled at him. 'Help yourself to pizza.'

'Thanks. Your grandfather sends his love, Izzy,' he said.

'He obviously liked you,' Izzy said with a grin. 'Did Rina give you a message for me?'

'She sends her r—love, too,' Liam said, but Izzy had already noticed the slip.

'What did she really say?' Izzy demanded.

He grimaced. 'Give my regards to Princess Isabella when you see her next.'

Izzy whistled. 'You clearly upset her.'

He wasn't going to tell her what he'd done. Instead, he made a noncommittal noise.

'Actually, it probably wasn't you.' Izzy pulled a face. 'Mamma's got it into her head that Rina needs to marry before she becomes

queen. She says there has to be a royal marriage and then the coronation.'

Liam damped down his instant reaction. Of
course it would be an arranged marriage. Vittoria di Sarda would have to get married for
political reasons. Even if she didn't, marriage
to a commoner would hardly go down well
with her people, would it?

And why was he even thinking about marriage and Vittoria, anyway? He didn't want
to get married to *anyone*, let alone a woman
he'd only met once. He'd been let down by too
many girlfriends who expected his undivided
attention. Maybe he'd just never managed to
pick Ms Right, who'd understand that his family and his career were both important to him;
but he was tired of feeling torn between his
love life, his career and his family.

'An arranged marriage?' Saoirse looked
shocked.

'Because she's going to be queen.' Izzy
folded her arms. 'And the man Mamma's suggested—he'd suffocate her. He's dull and all
he cares about is money and fast cars.'

So her husband wouldn't see the beautiful
princess sitting on the window seat and dreaming. He'd see the haughty woman in the Throne
Room.

'Mamma had probably been on at her all

morning about it and she'd had enough, and she took it out on you. I hope you didn't take it to heart if she did the Scary Winter Queen act on you.' Isabella sighed. 'Though I suppose that means Nonno got his stuffed waxwork.'

No way was he showing Izzy all the shots he'd taken, but he could soften it a bit for her. 'I took some shots in the Throne Room, as requested by your grandfather.' He smiled. 'And I asked your sister if I could take some in the library.'

'You really did take some for me?' Izzy beamed. 'Thank you. I'll make you coffee for the whole of the next week, for that.'

Liam couldn't hold back a smile. Izzy was irrepressible.

'So when do I get to see the shots?' Izzy asked.

'After your grandfather's approved them.'

Izzy rolled her eyes. 'This is my sister we're talking about.'

'And your grandfather is my client,' he reminded her, 'so he gets to see them first. If he chooses to share them with you, that's his decision. It's not mine to make.' Izzy's face fell, and he took pity on her. 'Here. These are the ones I took for you.' He handed her the prints.

She and Saoirse pored over them together in silence.

'Liam, I always knew you were good, but that's *stunning*,' Saoirse said at last. 'I think these are the best pictures you've ever taken.'

No, they weren't. But the evidence of *that* was staying private.

'I don't think I've ever seen such a beautiful picture of Rina.' Izzy fished out her favourite. 'In her happy place, too. She loves that library. And I...' Izzy swallowed hard. 'That's... Thank you. I'm not going to worry about the other pictures, now. Even though the pose might be stuffy, I know you won't have made her a waxwork. That's my sis—' She gulped the rest of the word off.

Saoirse hugged her. 'Iz. Now isn't the time to get homesick and be miserable. We have exams in a month.'

'I know. It's just... I *miss* her, Sursh. And it's my birthday next week.' She bit her lip. 'I know it's not special, like my twenty-first—' like Saoirse, Izzy had taken a couple of gap years before deciding on her university course '—but it still doesn't feel right not to spend the day with any of my family.'

Liam thought he must've gone temporarily insane, because the words came out before he could stop them. 'Why don't you see if your sister can juggle her schedule and come to London? Even if it's just for one day. And even if she can't, I'll cook you a birthday dinner and Saoirse will make you a birthday cake. We think of you as family,' he added gruffly.

'Liam, you're brilliant. Thank you.' Izzy hugged him. 'And you're family. You're the big brother I never had.'

'That's all sorted, then.' He wriggled out of the hug. 'I have work to do. See you later, girls.'

Liam didn't hear anything from the girls later in the week about Vittoria coming to see Izzy, so he assumed the schedule-juggling didn't work out. He also assumed that Izzy and Saoirse would want to go out with their friends on Izzy's birthday, so he arranged for Izzy to have dinner with them on the Monday night, the day before her birthday.

He marinaded chicken mini fillets in lemon juice before wrapping them in prosciutto and sage, prepped new potatoes for roasting, and asparagus and Cavalo Nero for steaming. He bought some of the first English strawberries along with shortbread thins and some clotted cream for pudding. Saoirse had made an incredibly rich chocolate cake and sprayed it with edible gold paint, and Liam had bought a cake fountain to top it. Saoirse had decorated their kitchen with birthday-themed bunting, and there was Prosecco chilling in the fridge.

Half an hour before Izzy was due to arrive, Saoirse came into the kitchen where Liam was sorting out last minute details, holding her mobile phone. 'You know you made extra chicken so Pietro could eat with us and you could have some cold for dinner tomorrow?'

'Uh-huh.'

'Could dinner stretch to two extra guests?'

All he'd have to do was prep some more veg. 'Yes. Why?'

'Vittoria's managed to come to London, after all. It's all been a bit last minute. Izzy doesn't want to dump us, because she knows you've gone to a lot of trouble to make a fuss of her. And she's worrying about asking you if her sister and her security detail can come for dinner, too, because she thinks she's being entitled.'

Vittoria di Sarda.

Here, in his flat.

Liam's heart skipped a beat.

'Tell Izzy it's fine,' he said, trying to sound as casual as he could.

He was glad that he had to spend time prepping more veg and re-laying the table, because that stopped him having time to think about Vittoria being here. Which was ridiculous in itself. He knew perfectly well that she wasn't coming here to see him; she was in London to see her sister. All he was doing was hosting dinner.

But he still remembered how Vittoria had looked in the library, in that moment when he'd almost kissed her, and anticipation prickled down his spine. How would it be when he saw her again? Would she be the formal queen-to-be or would her softer side come out because her little sister was here?

Half an hour later, the flat intercom buzzed, and Saoirse let their guests in.

Izzy came in and hugged Liam before introducing her sister and Giorgio, Vittoria's security detail.

Even though this was a relaxed dinner with her sister, Vittoria was wearing formal business dress—a navy dress with a matching jacket that Liam recognised from his studio work as haute couture, teamed with high-heeled court shoes and a little clutch bag. Her hair and make-up were immaculate; and her jewellery was minimal, diamond earrings and a simple pendant necklace.

She looked every inch a princess.

'Benvenuto nelle nostre casa, Vostre Altezza Reale,' Liam said with a small half-bow.

'Thank you, Mr MacCarthy,' she said, her voice equally formal.

Right. So it was definitely the princess rather than the girl in the library who was his guest. He'd make sure he behaved accordingly.

Izzy rolled her eyes. 'For pity's sake, you two. Stop being so stuffy. I know you've met on official palace business, but tonight *isn't* palace business, so let me introduce you properly. Rina, this is Liam, who's the nearest I'm going to get to a big brother. Liam, this is my big sister, Rina.' She gave both of them a steely look. 'Surely you get fed up to the back teeth of the formality at home, Rina? And as for you, Liam—' She shook her head in apparent despair. 'Don't treat my sister like some visiting dignitary.'

'Strictly speaking,' he pointed out, 'that's what she is.'

'She's my sister. Tonight's a sort of family dinner,' Izzy protested. 'And it's *my* birthday—'

'So you can act like a princess if you want to,' Liam teased.

She cuffed him. 'For that, I'm not letting Rina give you what she brought you.'

'Ah, now. Manners, young lady. We should always bring our host a gift when we're invited somewhere.'

Liam gave Vittoria a sidelong look. The love

for her sister in her eyes and her teasing expression were both vivid, and he itched to photograph her.

'Thank you for having us to dinner—may I call you Liam?' she asked. 'Izzy's right. Tonight isn't the night for formality.'

'Of course.' The way she spoke his given name made a shiver run down his spine.

'Good. And thank you especially for letting us come at such short notice,' Vittoria continued. 'It's not much of a gift, but we brought wine; and Izzy says you like cooking.'

'I do.'

She handed him a bottle of olive oil. 'This is from San Rocello. Extra-virgin, first pressing.'

Was she giving him an economist's spiel, or was she talking as someone who liked food and would spend time in the kitchen if she could? Izzy made great coffee, but always burned toast because she was too scatty to pay attention. But in that one photographic sitting he'd worked out that Vittoria paid attention to detail...

Then Liam made the mistake of looking into those amazing eyes. '*Grazie*, ma—' He stopped himself. She'd practically given him permission to use her first name. 'Thank you, Vittoria.'

For a moment, everyone else in the room

was forgotten: his sister, hers, Pietro and Giorgio. It was just the two of them. A heartbeat. Two. He almost reached out to take her hand…

And then he shook himself. 'May I offer you a drink? Dinner will be ready in ten minutes.'

He sorted out the drinks, seated everyone at the table and served dinner.

'Our grandfather was very pleased with the portraits you sent him,' Vittoria said.

'Good.' Which meant they would be used; and it was quite likely that one of them would end up in the National Portrait Gallery.

'And Izzy sent me the ones you took for her.'

His eyes met hers. Did she wonder what had happened to the photograph from that more private moment? Maybe he'd show her. But not now. 'Did you like them?' he asked instead.

'You're very talented,' she said.

Which wasn't the same as saying that she liked them. It was a diplomat's reply.

'Liam's really good,' Saoirse said.

'And dinner's getting cold,' he pointed out, hoping it would change the subject.

Everyone ate with gusto, to his relief. After everyone had finished pudding, he brought the birthday cake over to the table and lit the fountain candle, then they all sang 'Happy Birthday' to Izzy—himself and Saoirse in English, and Vittoria, Pietro and Giorgio switching to the Italian. *'Tanti auguri a te...'*

When the cake fountain had finished, Izzy closed her eyes to make a wish, then started cutting the cake.

'I'll make coffee to go with the cake,' Liam suggested.

'No! Anyone but *you* on coffee duty,' Izzy begged.

'My coffee isn't that bad,' Liam protested.

'Yes, it is. You microwave it when it gets cold. Your coffee is awful,' Saoirse agreed.

'*Really* awful. I'll make it,' Pietro said, and proceeded to sort it out.

'Don't be offended,' Vittoria said. 'Nobody's good at everything—and the chicken was quite delicious.'

Liam could tell she'd been well schooled in diplomacy. *Nobody's good at everything...* He wondered what she might not be good at, then pushed the thought away; it was none of his business.

'Happy birthday, piccola,' Vittoria said, and raised her glass of Prosecco in a toast to her little sister.

Izzy beamed. 'I'm so glad you're here, Rina. I didn't think you'd have time to see me, so I was thinking about skiving off and coming home for a couple of days.'

'Which isn't a good idea, so close to your exams. And of course I'd make time for you. I always will. You're my little sister and I love you.'

Vittoria couldn't help glancing at Liam; she could see in his face that he understood exactly where she was coming from. It was the same for him.

'I just wish Mamma wasn't putting all this pressure on you to get married,' Izzy said, frowning. 'It's utterly ridiculous. Why on earth do you have to get married before you become queen? This is the twenty-first century, not the sixteenth.'

'It's just how it is,' Vittoria said gently. Though she, too, wished she didn't have to get married. She knew it was her duty, and she'd do what was expected of her; but she wanted enough time to get to know her future partner and grow to at least respect him, if not fall in love with him, before they married.

What she'd seen of José so far didn't fill her with much hope. All they had in common was a royal background. He adored fast cars and sport, which bored her; and she liked exploring gardens and nature, which bored him.

'There's so much pressure on you,' Izzy continued. 'Once you get married and become queen, you'll lose the little freedom you have now. When was the last time you had some time to yourself?'

Vittoria thought about it and couldn't remember.

She'd clearly taken too long to answer, because Izzy pounced. 'Exactly. The palace suffocates you, Rina.'

Vittoria was going to deny it, but she knew her sister would call her on it. 'It's just how it is,' she said again.

'Why don't you take some time for yourself now?'

'Now?'

'While you're in London.' Izzy brightened. 'Like a modern-day *Roman Holiday*.'

Vittoria groaned. Her sister was a huge Audrey Hepburn fan, so Vittoria had ended up seeing the film a gazillion times. 'It's a lovely film, *piccola*, but it's of its time. Back in the nineteen-fifties, someone might notice a princess—but then they'd have to go and find a phone before they could tell the press about it, so the princess would have time to escape. Nowadays, almost everyone has a mobile phone, so they'd snap a picture or take a video, and it would be round the world in three seconds flat.' Which was why she had to be in strict control of every single second of every single day, making sure that the paparazzi never saw her frowning or bored or cross. She had an image to uphold.

'If you looked like you do right now,' Liam said, 'that's true. But if you didn't...'

That got her attention. She looked at him—and oh, those cornflower-blue eyes felt as if they could see into her soul.

'What are you saying?'

'Dress differently and change your hair. People might give you a second glance and think that you look a bit like Princess Vittoria—but then they'd see what you were wearing, realise that a princess wouldn't scruff around in chain store jeans and canvas shoes because she always wears a haute couture dress or suit and designer heels, and they'd move on. Leaving you in peace.'

Anonymity.

Given how much her mother was pressuring her right now, Vittoria really wanted a respite; it was why she'd carved time she didn't really have out of her schedule to come to London and see her sister, to grab a few little moments of joy to see the person she loved most in the world.

And now she was being offered a couple of days where she could be herself instead of a queen-in-waiting. Just a little time out before she stepped back into her real world.

'It'd be really easy to change your hair,' Izzy said.

'I can't cut it or dye it,' Vittoria warned.

'You don't need to,' Saoirse said. 'Remember what my brother does for a living. And he's done a few fashion shoots so he knows loads of people who work in wardrobe departments—people who can get you a wig. Something that'll suit your skin colouring but won't attract notice: say, mid-brown hair in a chin-length bob,' she added thoughtfully.

'You could borrow some clothes from me, or from Sursh,' Izzy added. 'We're all about the same size.'

'And you'll need contact lenses, because your gorgeous eyes are a giveaway,' Saoirse said. 'Brown eyes. They'll go with your colouring, too, and they're practically invisible.'

'Hang on, guys. Princess Vittoria can't just do things on a whim. She has a schedule,' Liam said.

Vittoria exchanged a glance with him. It seemed he understood her life. Then again, he also worked to a schedule and had the pressure of other people's deadlines—something their sisters were both yet to really experience.

Did he ever feel stifled by his job? Or, when

he'd shouldered the responsibility of bringing up his sister at the age of eighteen, had he felt trapped at the same time as loving her dearly? Because, right now, that was exactly how she felt: she loved her grandfather dearly and she would never shy away from her duty, but she needed some space. Just a little time for herself. Time where she could blend into the crowd, be just another one of the billions of people on the planet.

'You're meant to be on *our* side, Liam,' Izzy said, putting her hands on her hips and giving him a hard stare. 'You know someone who can sort out a wig and contact lenses by tomorrow morning, right?'

'Yes.'

'Well, then. Ring them. And you call Matteo Battaglia, Rina. Tell him you've got the worst period in the world so you need a couple of days off, and then you can have your *Roman Holiday*. Except, obviously, not in Rome,' Izzy added with a smile. 'It'd be a London holiday.'

Vittoria shook her head. 'The press already know I'm staying in your apartment. They'll look for me.'

'Then stay somewhere else.'

Vittoria rolled her eyes. 'I can hardly book somewhere incognito. No, Izzy, it's a lovely thought, and thank you so much—but it's completely unworkable.'

* * *

Liam knew he shouldn't really be encouraging the girls. But he'd seen that moment of longing in Vittoria's eyes, just before she masked it. He knew how it felt to shoulder greater responsibility than was normal for someone of your age and, while not resenting it, occasionally wanting to escape it and have some time for yourself.

He'd been lucky. Patty, his old tutor, had helped him out. Maybe it was time to pay it forward and give someone else a break. He could make this happen for Vittoria. Give her a respite, just a couple of days to step outside her royal bubble.

And neither of the security details had spoken up to say it was a ridiculous idea, so maybe Izzy's scheme wasn't quite so crazy after all.

'You could stay here, if you wish to stay in London. Or I can book you a suite somewhere, so there isn't a paper trail back to you.'

Vittoria turned to look at him, her face full of questions.

And that made him push it that little bit further. 'I also have a bolthole. A cottage by the sea. I was going there anyway this week to do some planning, so you're very welcome to join me. There's nothing like the sea to clear your head.'

'A cottage by the sea…'

'It has three bedrooms.' She didn't need to know that he used one of them as his darkroom. 'One for you, one for Giorgio—' he glanced at the bodyguard, who looked approving '—and one for me, so I can drive you there and maybe show you round the area if you'd like to explore, or stay out of your way if you just want time to yourself.'

A few days by the sea. Time for herself—something she wanted so very badly. It was so tempting.

This was only the second time she'd met Liam. Going to his cottage meant entrusting herself to a near-stranger. A man she found distractingly attractive. Which meant this was a bad idea.

On the other hand, he was clearly close to Izzy and treated her as part of his family. Izzy obviously trusted him, or she wouldn't have spoken so frankly in front of him. She already knew that Pietro approved of him—and the security detail would have raised any concerns with her grandfather before letting Izzy spend time in Liam's company.

Which meant he was safe.

So did she go with him, take those few days to recharge herself properly? Or did she do what she was supposed to and go back to the palace?

The sensible side of her knew that she should put her duties first. That wanting a break was self-indulgent—no, more than that, it was *selfish*.

But the part of her she usually kept hidden— the woman Liam had seemed to notice when he'd taken those photographs in the library— wanted to do it.

'Do it, Rina,' Izzy urged.

Vittoria looked at her sister and then back at Liam. 'If you're sure it's no trouble?'

He met her gaze. 'It would be my pleasure.'

There was nothing leering or anything that made her feel uncomfortable in his face. Just fellow feeling—as if he understood what it was like to feel constricted. And that decided her. 'Thank you. I'll talk to Matteo Battaglia.'

'Brilliant.' Izzy hugged her. 'This is going to change your life.'

CHAPTER THREE

AT A QUARTER to ten the next morning, Vittoria was ready to go. Izzy and Saoirse had both raided their wardrobes and lent her the kind of clothing that wouldn't attract a second glance: faded jeans, plain T-shirts and floral canvas pumps.

Liam had called in a couple of favours the previous evening and organised some people to come to Izzy's flat first thing, ostensibly as suppliers for a student art project, but in reality to sort out contact lenses and a wig for Vittoria's disguise. She knew they'd be discreet, because they were used to working with celebrity clients and keeping things private. She'd chosen brown contact lenses, on Saoirse's advice, and a mid-brown wig that looked natural with her skin tone.

The woman who stared back at her from the mirror wasn't the princess in haute couture and diamonds; she looked like any other professional woman in her late twenties who was getting away from the office for a few days.

'You look great. Normal,' Izzy said.

'Thank you.' Though Vittoria didn't feel normal. She felt strange. Borrowed clothes, borrowed hair and eyes... Didn't they say be careful what you wished for, in case you got it? She'd wanted anonymity. Now she had it. And it wasn't quite what she'd expected. It felt odd.

'I feel a bit bad, deserting you on your birthday,' she said.

Izzy laughed. 'This is the best birthday present ever. Knowing that you're actually going to unwind, for once. Anyway, you already celebrated with me last night.'

'I guess. As long are you're sure.'

Saoirse's phone beeped. 'That's Liam. He's waiting outside for you,' she said.

Izzy hugged her sister. 'We won't come down with you, in case the press twig who you are. Have fun and let me know when you're there safely.'

'I will.' Vittoria hugged her back. 'Thank you. Both of you.'

'We've hardly done anything. We just made a few suggestions and lent you some clothes. It's Liam who's actually sprung you from the public eye,' Izzy said.

And that was something Vittoria hadn't allowed herself to think about, because it was even more worrying. Spending a few days with the first man in years who'd made her feel something. Particularly as he wasn't from her background. Hadn't she learned anything from her experience with Rufus? Royal life was a lot to handle for people who hadn't been brought up in it. She couldn't afford to get emotionally involved with someone else who decided he didn't want that kind of life and would back away from her after she'd lost her heart to him.

She'd almost forgotten herself and kissed Liam in the palace library. In front of the footman, because right at that moment she hadn't been aware of anyone else in the room apart from Liam MacCarthy. What might happen in a little cottage by the sea? When Giorgio was in his room, and she and Liam were alone? She trusted Liam, but she wasn't entirely sure she trusted herself.

Was this all a mistake? Was she just being self-indulgent and pathetic, wanting a breather from her responsibilities? Should she say that she'd changed her mind? But everyone had gone to so much trouble to help her that it would feel churlish.

Her nerves grew as she followed Giorgio down the stairs from Izzy's flat.

'Liam's is the grey car, second on the right,' Giorgio said.

Well, of course Liam would have been in contact with her security detail and kept him informed about everything. Giorgio's presence and protection was about the only reason why her grandfather wouldn't be too angry with her when he found out about this—an escapade that would be instantly forgiven had it been Izzy, but the heir to the throne was expected to be much more sensible.

Again, she considered chickening out and going back to her real life.

But she'd felt so constrained, lately. So tired of being told what her duties were, and how she had to get married for the sake of the monarchy. She'd been longing to escape for *months*. Besides, this wasn't running away from her responsibilities for ever: she was simply stealing a couple of days by the sea. Days where she could just be *herself*.

There were a couple of photographers milling about outside. They'd clearly been tipped off that Princess Vittoria had come to visit her little sister; but Giorgio was good at making himself invisible, and the changes to her own appearance meant that none of them gave her a second glance as she slid into the passenger seat of Liam's car.

She was very fortunate that Liam wasn't the sort of man to insist on driving a bright red Ferrari or something similarly eye-catching. An anonymous grey car—even if it did seem to be top of the range—meant that they wouldn't have to run the gauntlet of the press.

'Thank you, Mr MacCarthy,' she said as she fastened her seatbelt.

He pushed his dark glasses up into his hair and looked at her. 'I thought we'd agreed on first-name terms? Actually, thinking about that, if I call you Vittoria it might make people put two and two together.'

'So I get a borrowed name as well as borrowed clothes?' This was a step too far.

'No. It needs to be something you'll recognise and react to. We could anglicise your name and shorten it slightly.' He smiled. 'Vicky.'

'Izzy calls me "Rina".'

'The press might pick up on that.'

'Oh.' She didn't have an answer to that. 'OK, I guess I'd better be "Vicky", then.'

'Feel free to change the music, Vicky,' he said with a smile, gesturing to the car's sound system.

'It's fine,' she said, and kept silent while he drove them out of London, guessing that he might want to concentrate on where they were going.

Once they were on the motorway heading north out of London towards East Anglia, he said, 'Let me know if you need a comfort break or want to stop for a drink.'

'Thank you.'

Funny, she had a whole stock of conversational openings designed to put people at their ease. But right now, she couldn't remember a single one of them; instead, when she opened her mouth, she found herself saying, 'So what's the village like?'

'It's a traditional fishing village—a harbour, lots of little fishermen's cottages and a wide sandy beach after the dunes.' He smiled. 'If you want a sneak preview, have a look on my website. The beach is the third one on the landscape gallery.'

There was a wide strip of sand that looked golden in the sunlight, darkening as it neared the edge of the sea; a froth of white showed the waves lapping onto the shore, and the sea graduated from turquoise in the shallows through to almost navy at the horizon. The sky was filled with storm clouds, deep and dramatic grey. 'That's gorgeous.'

'It was a lucky shot,' he said. 'The sun lit up the sand from behind me, and it was the perfect contrast to the sky. Sometimes you just happen to be in the right place at the right time.' He paused. 'So, is there anything particular you'd like to do in your few days of escape?'

'I don't know,' she said. It had been so long since she'd had a real choice in what she did, she wasn't sure where to start. 'What sort of thing do you normally do?'

'Walk, work and think,' he said. 'Though I've lent the cottage to my best friend and his family in the past. I spent some time here with them last summer, so the order of the day was making sandcastles on the beach. We went out on a boat trip to see the seals, and we've gone hunting for shells and fossils.' He gave her a sidelong look. 'What do you normally do at the beach?'

She couldn't remember the last time she'd been to the beach just for fun. It was always something to do with conservation, heritage or tourism. 'I don't usually have time to go to the beach.'

'This is your *Roman Holiday*, Vittoria,' he said gently. 'You can do whatever you want.'

She'd got exactly what she'd wished for.

And, now there were no boundaries, it was faintly scary.

She was so used to working with royal protocols; but here, there were no protocols. She wasn't quite sure what to say or do. She and

Liam barely knew each other; they didn't have a shared history or shared references.

Or maybe she was overthinking this. Maybe they *did* have a shared frame of reference—he'd been a parent to his little sister at the age of eighteen, and she was about to become queen at the age of twenty-eight. So many responsibilities at such a young age; maybe he'd guessed that she was struggling and he was helping her because he'd been there, too.

This was a step outside her usual life. Something to refresh and revitalise her, to help her cope with the parts of the palace that she found stifling.

An adventure.

So she should just stop worrying and enjoy it.

It took them three hours to get there, but finally Liam parked in the driveway of a pretty flint and brick cottage. 'My neighbour who keeps an eye on the place when nobody's here promised to pick up some milk, bread and a few bits from the deli,' he said, opening the door and ushering her into the kitchen.

There was a deep red flagstone floor; the walls were painted pale blue and the cupboards were cream. There was an old-fashioned butler's sink underneath the window and a range cooker nearby. The room was large enough to have a scrubbed pine table and chairs at one end; it looked very much like a family room. Normal. Everyday. All the things she didn't usually have.

It didn't take long to view the rest of the house. Next was the living room, with a wood-burning stove, comfortable sofas, and stripped oak floorboards with a patterned red rug in the centre. A steep staircase led to the next floor, which had two rooms—one was a darkroom and one had a double bed—plus a bathroom. There was a second flight of stairs which led to another bedroom which had a wide double bed, a view of the sea and an en-suite shower room.

This was exactly where she could imagine having a bolthole.

'It's a lovely house,' she said. But there was one thing bothering her. He'd said there were three bedrooms. She'd only seen two.

'Choose whichever bedroom you'd like,' Liam said.

She really would have to say something now. 'But there are only two.'

'One of them doubles as my darkroom. I'll sleep there on the sofa bed.'

She shook her head. 'I can't ask you to do that.'

'It's what I normally do if I have friends staying,' he said. 'It's fine.'

'Then, if you're sure, I'd like the room on the top floor, please.' She'd loved it at first sight: it was light and airy.

'Good choice,' Liam said. 'The view first thing is gorgeous. I'll leave you to freshen up while I sort out lunch.'

'I'll bring everything in from the car,' Giorgio said, and Liam handed over his car keys with a smile of thanks.

Her surroundings were much simpler than what she was used to, but utterly charming. The whole place had a feeling of warmth—a feeling of *family*. Like rare days at the palace when her mother and grandmother had gone to see friends, and she could walk around the gardens with her grandfather, as she'd once done with her father, have a simple lunch with him and forget the weight of her future crown. Or when Izzy was home and she managed to get time off, so they could both curl up on the window seat in her room and talk…

Giorgio brought up her bags; she thanked him, called Izzy to let her know they'd arrived and the cottage was lovely, unpacked, then freshened up and went downstairs.

Liam had laid the table in the kitchen with salad, fresh bread, cheese, ham and what looked like dressed crab.

'It's all local produce,' he said. 'Even the coffee's roasted by the local deli.'

'And I didn't let him make the coffee, so it's safe to drink,' Giorgio said with a grin.

Vittoria noticed that her bodyguard had already become friendly with Liam, to the point where they were comfortable teasing each other. It was a good thing; but it was also unsettling, because she wasn't sure what her own relationship was with Liam. They were acquaintances—she knew he was close to her sister—and she thought they could easily become friends. She liked him instinctively. But he was also a man who made her feel things she couldn't afford to feel, and she needed to get herself back under control. Fast.

'This all looks delicious—thank you,' she said. 'But I don't expect you to wait on me, and I'll do the washing up.'

He raised an eyebrow.

Did he *really* think she was that spoiled and privileged? That stung. 'Yes, I do know how to wash up. I fended for myself when I was a student,' she said coolly.

'I apologise. I didn't mean to assume that you were helpless.'

But he clearly had made that assumption. 'And I can cook,' she said. 'I like cooking; I just don't get the chance to do it much.'

'Then if you'd like to cook while you're here, do it,' he said.

And that took all her defensiveness away.

This man had been kind enough to help give her a couple of days of freedom from the pressure of always being on show in her normal life; yet she'd snapped at him. 'Sorry. I didn't mean to be snippy with you.'

'It's fine,' he said.

She really hoped that wasn't pity in his eyes.

'So what would you like to do after lunch?' he asked.

'Could we go for a walk on the beach, then pick up some shopping for dinner?'

'Sure—unless you'd rather eat fish and chips on the quayside tonight,' he said. 'Your choice.'

Like a tourist. Eating fish and chips from the wrapper, with their feet dangling over the edge of the quay. And nobody would see the princess: she'd be just like everyone else.

And it was her choice. She didn't have to think what would be best politically; she could do whatever she wanted, just for the sheer joy of it.

'There are plenty of options,' he said. 'We could have fish and chips tonight, or go to the pub, or one of us can cook dinner. If you want to go exploring somewhere, we can eat on the way home. Whatever you like.'

How long had it been since she'd been able to choose?

'I think I'd like fish and chips tonight,' she said. 'But I'm still doing the washing up after lunch.'

'Fine. Then I'll dry,' he said.

There was something fragile about Vittoria di Sarda, beneath her cool royal exterior, Liam thought. Although she was a princess, she didn't behave as if she was entitled—unlike some of his past girlfriends, who'd demanded more than he'd been prepared to give.

Not that he should be thinking about her in terms of being a girlfriend. He could list half a dozen reasons off the top of his head why getting involved with her would be a bad idea—for them both. She was his guest. He ought to leave it at that.

After lunch, they headed for the beach, with Giorgio strolling a few paces behind them, looking like any other tourist checking his phone but in reality finely tuned to any situation that could become difficult for the princess. Liam had already had a long chat with Vittoria's security detail, the previous evening, briefing him about the area and any potential risks. Given that the English royal family had houses only a few miles away, Giorgio was relatively relaxed.

In the first part of the beach they reached, there were small children playing with buckets and spades, and Liam noticed Vittoria looking wistfully at them.

'Didn't you do that sort of thing when you were small?' he asked.

'It feels like a very long time ago, now,' she said. She frowned. 'You're a couple of years older than me. Doesn't it feel like a long time ago to you?'

'No, because I still build sandcastles with my goddaughters—my best friend Olly's girls,' he said. 'And sometimes Olly and I get a bit competitive and see who can build the most ornate castle.'

'Men,' she said, rolling her eyes.

How weird it was, Liam thought, that even though she didn't look the same—she didn't even have the same eye colour, thanks to the contact lenses she was using—she still made his heart skip a beat. The more time he spent with her, the more he liked her. The more attractive he found her. The more he wanted to be with her.

But she was off limits. He really needed to keep remembering that.

He took his shoes off so he could walk along

the edge of the sea; she did the same, dangling the canvas shoes by their laces as she walked along.

'I can't remember the last time I walked barefoot on a beach, with the waves washing over my toes,' she said.

'The beach is a good place. The sound of the sea can drive all the worries from your head,' he said.

'Is this what you do when you're out of sorts?'

'Pretty much,' he said. 'I'll come here with my camera, listen to the waves and the birds, and take a few shots to ground me again.' He looked at her. 'Given that you live on an island, I'm surprised you don't walk on the beach more often. Don't you have a special royal beach?'

'No—as you already know from your visit, the palace is in the capital. Although there's a port, there isn't a beach you can walk on.' She shrugged. 'There's always the garden.'

'Or the library.'

Again, her gaze met his and it sent a frisson of desire down his spine. He could still see the woman he'd photographed on the window seat, her face all soft in the diffused light. The woman he'd almost kissed. The woman he was tempted to kiss right now: but he held himself back.

'Why do you take portraits rather than landscapes?' she asked.

'Partly for commercial reasons—I get more commissions for portraits than I would for landscapes—and partly because I like the challenge of showing someone's character through an image,' he answered honestly.

'But you take landscapes when you're out of sorts. Is that your dream, to be a landscape photographer?'

'No. I want to be one of the greatest portrait photographers of my generation,' he said.

'*Nonno* was impressed with the photographs you took. I saw them, too: they're good.' She looked him straight in the eye again. 'But he only showed me a single one from the library. Where I was still wearing royal regalia.'

'Because the others weren't the ones he commissioned. Izzy asked me to take a photograph for her—and I took several.'

Her eyes narrowed slightly. 'But you took more than the ones she showed me.'

'When you were quoting Shakespeare,' he said. 'There's one—' He stopped.

'Can I see it?'

'It's not going to be used anywhere. You have my word on that.'

She was silent.

'Vittoria,' he said softly. 'I keep my promises.'

'I imagine you do, Mr MacCarthy.'

She'd gone all cold and regal on him. Which he probably deserved.

'Nobody else has seen it. Not even Izzy.'

She inclined her head. 'However, given that it's of me, I think I have a right to see it.'

She had a point. He sighed. 'All right. Give me a moment.' He checked the signal, then logged in to his cloud-based storage. Then he fished out a single picture. The one he'd taken when he'd finished the sonnet for her. Without comment, he handed her his phone.

She stared at the portrait.

And he could see the colours changing in her face as she looked at it—first pale, then a deep blush.

'Oh,' she said, her voice all soft and breathy.

'It's the best picture I've ever taken,' he said. 'Without question. It's a career-changing shot.' He waited a beat before adding, 'And I'm not intending to publish it.' Because that moment was too private. It revealed almost as much about the photographer as it did about his subject: and he hoped she hadn't worked that out for herself.

'I…' Her eyes were wide. 'I don't know what to say.'

'Then don't say anything. Just keep walking along the beach,' he said, and held out his hand for his phone.

She looked at the portrait once more, then gave his phone back.

'Thank you,' he said, logging out of his storage space and then stuffing the phone back in his pocket.

They walked on without speaking. As they walked on the sand and the sound of the sea worked its usual magic on him, he found the silence between them slide from being awkward to being relaxed.

Vittoria was completely stunned by that photograph. It felt as if Liam had captured the inner her, the one she had to mask when she was a queen-in-waiting. The woman who dreamed, who looked up at the stars and wondered at the universe.

She'd never really felt before that someone understood her and saw who she was inside, even Rufus. Certainly not José, the man that her mother was pressuring her to accept as her husband and future consort. He was handsome and had been brought up in royal circles; but he didn't make her heart beat faster and she hadn't felt an emotional connection to him.

Though she knew her duty and she'd do what

was expected of her: marry a suitable man and produce the next heir to the throne.

All she needed was a little time to steel herself for that duty.

Her hand brushed against Liam's as they walked, and it felt as if she'd been galvanised.

Why was she so aware of him?

She'd never reacted like this to anyone before. Not the couple of boyfriends she'd had in her late teens, and not Rufus.

Vittoria had promised herself that she'd never make the mistake she made with Rufus again. She'd marry someone who'd grown up in the same sort of world that she had and could deal with all the media intrusion. Maybe it was a little too much to ask that she could fall in love with him, first.

Liam took her hand, squeezed it and let it go.

She looked at him, shocked. 'Why did you do that?'

'Because right then you looked really sad,' he said softly, 'and I'm not sure if I'm allowed to give you a hug.'

'How do you mean, allowed?'

'Protocol.'

So, even though this was meant to be her time out of being a princess, there were still the same boundaries. She frowned. 'Do you hug Izzy?'

'I have done, in the past. Purely in a brotherly way,' he added, 'when she's had a rubbish day and needed the equivalent of a big brother to tell her that everything would work out just fine.'

It was the sort of thing she would've done, had he been the prince and Saoirse had been the one to need a hug. And in the short time she'd known Liam she'd started to realise that he saw the world in much the same way that she did. Pragmatic, practical, doing what needed to be done without a fuss. Of course he would've hugged Izzy when she needed it.

Then she found herself wondering what it would be like if Liam hugged her... Except she didn't want a hug from him in a brotherly way.

For pity's sake.

This was meant to be a respite, not time to have a wild fling with her little sister's best friend's brother.

But now the idea was firmly lodged in her head and she couldn't get it out.

She let her hand brush deliberately against his a couple of times; the touch sent a frisson of desire through her. But she noticed that he didn't take the hint and didn't hold her hand. It made her feel like an embarrassed teenager trying desperately to get the boy she liked to notice her, and being turned down.

She thought about it.

He'd said just now that the hand-squeeze had been all about comfort; but she remembered the look in his eyes in the palace library, when he'd whispered Shakespeare to her and she'd thought he was going to kiss her. Comfort? No. She rather thought it had been something else. The same thing that was making her feel so antsy. Longing. Need. *Desire.*

So what was holding him back now? And how could she take that barrier away?

She shook herself. This wasn't sensible. And she was sensible, businesslike Princess Vittoria, who was simply pretending to be carefree tourist Vicky. She needed to remember that.

Even though she had to try really hard to suppress that prickling awareness—and didn't succeed completely—Liam MacCarthy was easy to be with. The silence between them as they walked along the beach, watching dogs racing around, was companionable rather than awkward. He was giving her space, and she appreciated that.

Then a large black Labrador rushed over, so intent on playing chase with another dog that he banged into her, nearly knocking her over.

Liam caught her and stopped her from falling, holding her close to him.

She could feel the warmth of his skin

through his T-shirt, and it made her tingle all over.

'Are you OK?' he asked.

She nodded, not trusting herself to speak because she knew her voice would come out all wobbly: a wobbliness that had nothing to do with the near-accident and everything to do with the fact that he was holding her.

'I'm so sorry,' the dog's owner called, 'I'm afraid the boys get a bit carried away as soon as their paws hit the sand. The little one's ten months old and has no sense whatsoever. Are you all right?'

'No harm done,' Liam called back.

'Thank you for catching me,' she said when she finally trusted herself to speak.

'You're welcome.'

And was it her imagination, or was there something in his blue eyes—that same awareness she had towards him?

By the time they walked back to the harbour, a queue was forming outside the chip shop.

'Why don't you wait here with Giorgio while I wait in line?' Liam suggested.

'I need to give you the mon—' she began, and he shook his head.

'Buying fish and chips for three isn't going to bankrupt me. It's fine. Cod and chips all right with you, Vicky?'

She knew she should give in gracefully. 'Thank you.'

'Giorgio?' Liam checked.

'Yes, please,' the bodyguard said.

'Great. Find somewhere to sit, and I'll come and find you with dinner.'

Vittoria sat down on the low harbour wall next to Giorgio and waited for Liam's return. The view across the salt marshes was amazing; there were a few boats moored up on the harbour, and the long sea wall stretched out towards the beach. Couples and families were sitting on the harbour wall, too, eating fish and chips; the children all seemed to be fascinated by the gulls, who stalked up and down the quayside, gimlet-eyed, waiting for someone to drop a chip so they could swoop in and grab it.

Nobody paid her the slightest bit of attention.

How good it felt to be able to merge into the crowd. To be just a normal person. Not to have to school her expression and mask her thoughts all the time.

'OK?' Giorgio asked softly.

She nodded.

'He's one of the good guys,' Giorgio said. 'I'm glad you agreed to Izzy's plan.'

'Nonno's not going to be pleased, when he finds out,' she said, wrinkling her nose.

'He'll be fine. He'll understand.'

She knew what her security detail wasn't saying. The ones who'd make a fuss about the situation were her mother and her grandmother: the ones who were pressuring her to agree on terms with José and organise the official engagement.

'Put it all out of your head. You can deal with it later. Just enjoy having time off—time for *you*,' Giorgio advised.

He'd been her security detail for nearly ten years, since she'd gone to London as an undergraduate; she knew his words of advice were meant kindly. And it was good advice. 'I will,' she said. Except it was much easier said than done.

They sat just enjoying the view and chatting about nothing in particular until Liam returned with three boxes of hot cod and chips. 'I hope it's OK, but I added salt and vinegar to all of them, because that's the best way to enjoy fish and chips,' he said, handing them each a box, a wooden fork and a paper napkin. 'And I played safe with drinks and bought us each a bottle of still water.'

'Lovely. Thank you so much,' she said.

'My pleasure.' His smile made her heart feel as if it had just done a backflip.

Summer, sunshine and the sea. Along with his nearness, it was a heady combination.

Not wanting to say anything else in case she started sounding like a starry-eyed teenager, Vittoria concentrated on the food. The chips were perfect: hot, crispy with the tang of salt and vinegar. The fish was beautifully fresh, the batter light, and she could see exactly why the queue outside the shop was so long.

When they'd finished, Giorgio bought them all a whippy ice-cream with a flake.

Just like all the other tourists.

She blended in.

And she enjoyed lingering on the quayside, laughing and chatting and people-watching, without the worry that someone was going to spot Princess Vittoria of San Rocello in the middle of it all and turn the whole thing into a media scrum. The pressure, the weight that seemed permanently between her shoulders and made her head ache most nights, started to ease.

By the time they got back to the cottage, it was beginning to get chilly.

'Are you tired?' Liam asked. 'Or would you like to walk back over to the dunes and watch the stars come out?'

'I think I'd like that,' she said. 'But let me grab Izzy's fleece, first.'

'Sure.'

'I'll stay here,' Giorgio said. 'I trust Liam to keep you safe, but you know what to do if there's a problem.'

She nodded. 'The panic button.'

By the time she'd come downstairs, Liam had sorted out two thermal mugs of hot chocolate and a blanket to sit on, which he stuffed into a tote bag and slung over his shoulder. They walked out to the dunes where he spread the blanket out and handed her a mug after she'd sat down. She could see the first stars appearing, and a narrow crescent moon hung above them, reflecting on the surface of the sea. The swish of the waves on the shore and the sound of birdsong were all they could hear. It was utterly magical. Though it was also cold, and neither the hot drink nor Izzy's fleece was quite enough to keep her warm. Liam must have noticed her shiver, because he shrugged off his jacket and put it round her shoulders.

'Won't you be cold?' she protested, feeling guilty.

'I'm fine.' He paused. 'Though if you want to lean against me, we could share some body heat.'

Every nerve-end prickled.

Was this Liam's way of saying he wanted to hold her? Would he kiss her? Vittoria could hardly breathe. All she'd have to do was turn slightly, tip her face up to his…

Or was he doing this in a completely platonic way, just being kind to the older sister of his little sister's best friend?

She was unsure about the situation—or about what she wanted it to be.

Move closer, or stay distant?

CHAPTER FOUR

THAT HAD BEEN a really stupid move, Liam thought.

What had he been thinking, asking Vittoria to move closer, to share their body heat?

He sounded like a teenager on his first date. Awkward, socially inept, and cringe-makingly embarrassing.

When his sister found out—which she would, when Vittoria told Izzy and Izzy told Saoirse—she'd kill him.

But then he felt the sand shift under the blanket as Vittoria shuffled slightly closer to him.

And it just seemed natural to slide his arm round her shoulders. Gently. Lightly.

She slid her arm round his waist, and for a second he couldn't breathe.

They were from different worlds. Of course this was never going to work out between them. He shouldn't even start something he knew they couldn't finish. A fling was out of the question. Someone in Vittoria's position couldn't just have a mad fling.

But he really, really wanted her. He couldn't remember the last time he'd wanted someone so much.

But then he made another mistake: he stole a glance at her.

She was looking up at him, her face sweet and guileless in the moonlight.

He forgot who she was, where they were. All he could see was a woman next to him in the moonlight, lifting her face to his for a kiss. The woman he'd wanted to kiss on the window seat of her library, all soft and sweet and taking his breath away. The woman who was right here in his arms.

It was impossible to resist.

He lowered his head until his lips brushed hers. Once. Twice. His mouth tingled where it touched hers. She tasted of hot chocolate and salty sea air and something sweet that was just her, and he wanted more.

Then she slid her free hand round his neck; the arm she'd wrapped round his waist drew him closer. And Liam was completely lost; nothing existed except kissing Vittoria. It felt as if he'd waited his whole life for this moment, where her mouth was claiming his and she was holding him as tightly as he was holding her.

There was a shout from further down the beach which jolted him back to the present. In one horrible moment, he realised where he was. Who he was kissing. And why he shouldn't be doing anything of the sort.

He broke away from her. 'I'm sorry. I shouldn't have...'

Colour slashed across her cheekbones. 'It's OK. We'll just pretend it didn't happen.'

Yeah, right. He had a feeling he'd be lying awake tonight until stupid o'clock, thinking about her and that kiss.

But he went along with it. 'Sure.' He didn't dare look her in the eye. 'We probably ought to go back.'

He got to his feet, waited for her to stand up, then sorted out the blanket and travel mugs.

'Don't you want your jacket?' she asked.

'No, it's fine. I'll be warm enough walking.'

This time, the silence between them as they walked back to the cottage was awkward. He didn't know how to fix it. Why had he been so stupid and given in to the urge to kiss her?

The worst thing was, now he knew what it felt like to kiss her, he wanted to do it all over again. And he knew he shouldn't.

Back in the kitchen, Giorgio was reading

the newspaper at the table with a mug of coffee beside him. He looked up as they walked in. 'Did you have a good walk?'

'Yes. But all this sea air has made me sleepy,' Vittoria said, and smothered a yawn that Liam was pretty sure was fake. 'I hope you'll excuse me.'

'Of course. Sleep well,' Giorgio said with a fond smile.

Liam didn't quite want to leave it like this. They still had another couple of days here, and he wanted them to be good ones, not filled with awkwardness because of his stupid mistake. 'I meant to say, earlier—the weather's meant to be good, so perhaps you'd like to go to see the seals tomorrow? There's a huge colony of common and grey seals a bit further round the coast, at Blakeney Point. It's quite a popular sight.'

'I remember—you said you'd gone last year with your best friend and his family.' She spread her hands. 'If it's OK with Giorgio, that'd be nice.'

Liam looked at the security detail. 'Risk assessment time?'

'Risk assessment time,' Giorgio agreed.

'We'll talk it over,' Liam said. 'If Giorgio's happy, I'll book tickets online and we'll go after breakfast tomorrow.' He had to suppress the sudden vision of waking in Vittoria's arms, because that definitely wasn't going to happen.

That kiss on the beach had been a mistake, and it wasn't going to be repeated—no matter how much he wanted it to.

'See you tomorrow,' she said, and left the kitchen.

Back in her room, Vittoria took off the wig and removed the contact lenses before showering and changing into a pair of pyjamas covered in sunflowers. The design was so very Izzy, and she felt a sharp pang, missing her little sister.

Izzy, too, had been instrumental in Vittoria's escape.

Today had been so very different from the kind of days she usually spent. No pressure, no having to be diplomatic—except for the moment when Liam had shown her the final photograph he'd taken in the library, and she'd had to mask her instant reaction. She'd looked as if she was about to be kissed, her expression all soft and dreamy and her lips parted. She hadn't looked like a princess; she'd looked like a woman dreaming of her lover.

Or a woman wondering what it would be like if a man she'd only just met kissed her.

She'd wondered.

And now she knew.

She'd been kissed in passion before. Kissed tentatively. Kissed by the man she'd thought she loved.

But nothing had felt like Liam MacCarthy's mouth against hers. Once definitely wasn't enough.

What was she going to do?

She'd told Liam and Giorgio that she wanted an early night. She'd fibbed that the sea air had made her sleepy; considering that she lived on an island and was very used to sea air, it had been a very stupid comment and they would both have known she was lying. Lying to herself, too, because she had a feeling she was going to spend most of the night awake, thinking about Liam MacCarthy and remembering the touch of his lips. Wishing she could kiss him all over again.

But she had a duty to fulfil. OK, she wasn't officially dating José, but she knew their families were trying to negotiate terms for a marriage. She couldn't afford to let herself fall for someone she definitely couldn't have, so she needed to keep Liam MacCarthy at a distance. No matter how much she wished that things could be different.

* * *

On Wednesday morning, there was a knock on Vittoria's door.

'Yes?' she called, sitting up in bed and pulling the duvet respectably round her.

The door opened a crack and she heard Giorgio's voice. 'Liam's booked the tickets for the seal trip. We need to leave in three-quarters of an hour.'

'OK. I'll be ready,' she said. With the wig and the contact lenses, she didn't need to worry about her hair or make-up. Even though she'd learned to be quick and flawless with cosmetics, it was nice to be able to choose *not* to wear any make-up without worrying what the press would say and what kind of spin there would be on the story—most probably about the princess looking ill, and then the suggestion that being queen would be too much for her.

'Liam's making bacon sandwiches,' Giorgio added, 'and I'm making coffee.'

'Wonderful. Give me fifteen minutes.'

Ten minutes later, she went downstairs in jeans, a T-shirt and the floral canvas shoes.

'Morning, Vicky.' Liam greeted her cheerfully, as if that kiss last night had never happened and neither had the awkwardness.

Even though she hadn't been able to stop thinking about that kiss, now wasn't the time or the place to discuss it. So she followed his lead. 'Morning, Liam.'

He slid a plate in front of her with a bacon sandwich cut neatly into triangles. 'Help yourself to ketchup or brown sauce.'

She smiled. 'I'll leave mine unadulterated, thanks. This looks lovely.' She tried to imagine José making her breakfast in their private apartment, and failed dismally. Whereas she could easily imagine Liam making waffles with maple syrup, or cooking eggs Florentine, or toasting cinnamon bagels.

Tough.

Liam wasn't going to be part of her future. She'd just have to find a way to fall in love with José.

But Vittoria's resolution failed miserably later that morning, when Liam had driven them further down the coast to catch the boat. He'd insisted on her wearing sunscreen plus Izzy's sunhat—a white floppy bucket hat covered in roses—and Giorgio helped her into the boat. Somehow she ended up sitting between him and Liam, and when the last people got onto the boat they all had to move up a little. Vittoria was very aware of the press of Liam's thigh against hers. He stretched one arm out behind her, to give her a little more room, and rested his other hand on the edge of the boat.

It would be so easy to move in closer to him. Though she intended to keep a tight control of her feelings and stay exactly where she was, with just enough distance between them.

They listened to the skipper going through the safety briefing. The boat was sailing smoothly and she'd got herself back under control when they hit a rough patch of water, the boat rocked unexpectedly, and she ended up practically falling into Liam. His arm tightened round her, keeping her safe; except she noticed that when they were sailing smoothly again he didn't move his arm away.

Should she move?

Stupid question. Of course she should.

But she didn't want to. And this was her sort-of *Roman Holiday*, her stolen time away. So it didn't count, did it?

She stayed right where she was, in the protective circle of his arm, enjoying his nearness.

The boat's skipper was telling them all about the area and what they were going to see, though Vittoria was so aware of Liam's proximity that she found it hard to concentrate.

They drew nearer to the spit of land in the distance. A blue building with white windows, a semi-circular roof and an observation tower came into view, and the skipper told them that it used to be the lifeboat shed but was now the visitor centre. There were lots of seabirds flying about; the skipper taught them the differences between the varieties of gulls and told them what to look out for.

As they moved further along the shingle and sand spit, the seals came into view, basking in the sun; many of them turned their faces to look at the boat, as if they were as intrigued by the occupants as the passengers were with them. One or two raised a flipper, as if waving. They had such pretty faces, with those huge dark eyes, smiling mouth and long whiskers; Vittoria's heart melted.

One or two of the seals shuffled off the sand, moving surprisingly fast; once in the water they immediately changed from slightly ungainly creatures to agile swimmers, ducking beneath the waves and popping up again to look at the boats.

'Don't crowd to the starboard side of the boat,' the skipper warned. 'You'll all get the same opportunities to take photographs, because we'll be returning the same way and the port side will get the better view on the way back.'

People on the starboard side of the boat, closest to the seals, were snapping photos.

Liam surprised her by taking his phone from his pocket. 'Budge up, Giorgio—we'll take a selfie to send to Izzy,' he said, keeping his voice low so he didn't ruin the commentary for the other passengers.

'You use a *phone* camera?' she asked, keeping her own voice low. 'When you're... A professional photographer?'

He smiled. 'The best camera is always the one that's to hand. Sure, a phone doesn't have the same flexibility as an SLR, but I'm never going to be snobby about it.' He took a couple of shots. 'You can choose which one you want to send her later.'

'Thanks.' She took some pictures of the seals on her phone and reviewed them.

The disappointment must've shown on her face, because he said softly, 'What's wrong?'

She shrugged. 'I wanted to capture the expressions on the seals' faces. These are a bit too far away.'

He took a camera from his pocket, checked one of the settings and handed it to her. 'Try this.'

He was offering her his camera? But this was what he did for a living. Wasn't this an expensive, precious piece of kit? 'But isn't it—?' she began.

'It's a digital compact camera,' he said. 'It's old and battered and very reliable. It's the one I keep in my pocket if I'm not going somewhere specifically to shoot something. I also use it when I'm checking out the background for a shoot. I've set it on auto mode, so you don't have to spend time focusing the shot.' He showed her how to use the zoom.

'Thank you. Though it's a bit intimidating, taking photographs next to a professional.'

He shook his head. 'Ignore what I do for a living. Take the shot that pleases you. There are rules that can help you take better compositions, yes; but we can go through those another time, if you want to. For now, just keep it simple, use the zoom if you want close-ups, and look at the details that interest you. I'll send you the pictures over Wi-Fi when we get back.'

'Thank you.'

Finally she got the pictures she wanted. Her hand touched his when she gave the camera back to him, sending a surge of awareness through her, and she was glad of the sunglasses that meant he couldn't read her feelings in her eyes. Though his glasses meant that she couldn't read his feelings, either.

Princess Vittoria di Sarda was cool, confident and collected. She'd been trained for years not to let any situation throw her. The woman sitting on a boat full of tourists, with borrowed clothes and a borrowed name, didn't feel in the slightest bit cool or collected. She felt like a teenager with a crush on a friend's big brother. And it threw her completely.

Liam didn't slide his arm round her on the journey home, and she wasn't sure if that was more of a relief or a disappointment. It was definitely a mixture of the two. Relief, because it gave her the space to get her thoughts collected again; disappointment, because she liked his nearness.

She focused on the skipper's commentary all the way back to the harbour, and Giorgio was the one who held her hand to steady her while she climbed off the boat and back onto the quayside.

They had a simple lunch in a little pub with the most amazing sea views, then Liam drove them further round the coast to another beach. 'I'm guessing that looking in tide pools and beach-combing for fossils isn't part of your everyday life.'

'No. It's not something I ever really remember doing,' she admitted.

He glanced at her canvas shoes. 'They should be fine. You're sensible enough to realise the rocks will be a bit slippery and be careful where you put your feet.'

Vittoria thoroughly enjoyed looking in the tide pools, spotting crabs, anemones, limpets

and starfish. She took a few shots on her phone
for Izzy.

On the way back to the car, they beach-
combed for fossils.

'So what kind of fossils are we looking for?'
she asked.

'Sponges and coral. Or a belemnite.'

'What's that?'

'Apparently it was a bit like a squid but had
a hard skeleton. Look for an amber stone that
looks a bit like a bullet casing, and is about the
length of your thumb.'

They continued looking, and Vittoria bent
to pick up a cylinder-shaped stone. 'Do you
think this is a belemnite?' she asked, handing
it to him. Her fingers tingled when her skin
touched his.

'Definitely.' He smiled at her and dropped
it back into her palm. 'Well spotted.'

Again, at the brief touch of his skin, she felt
that weird tingling. 'There are three or four
others here,' she said. 'But someone else might
enjoy finding them, so I'm not going to take
more than one.'

His smile was full of approval and made her
feel warm all over.

They called into a supermarket on the way
back to the cottage to buy the makings of din-

the traditional ridges on one side and a thumb-print on the other.

When she'd cooked dinner as a student, it had been fun rather than a chore—a kind of balance to studying hard.

When had life stopped being fun?

She would never shirk her duty, but these stolen days had shown her that she needed a little more balance in her life.

Once she'd made the gnocchi, she sliced strawberries and set them to steep in balsamic vinegar and black pepper; then she sliced up mozzarella, plum tomatoes and avocado and arranged them on three plates and decorated them with a tiny drizzle of pesto. Funny how such a simple thing could make her feel so good.

She laid the table, then called Liam and Giorgio in from the garden.

They were both appreciative of the meal.

'It wasn't exactly difficult. The first course and pudding were really just assembly jobs,' she pointed out.

'But you made the pesto and gnocchi yourself. You could've just bought some ready-made from the chiller cabinet at the su-permarket,' Liam said. 'And this is the best pesto I've ever tasted. Really fresh and zingy.'

The compliment warmed her all the way

ner. Liam insisted on taking the basket before they got to the checkout.

'This isn't fair. You paid for dinner last night.'

'We don't want a paper trail leading back to you, remember,' he said softly. 'And if I was in London I'd be buying groceries. So this is pretty much the same thing.'

She couldn't argue with him. But she could send him a thank-you gift once she was back in San Rocello. A first edition of his favourite book, perhaps, or a piece of art. He'd given her time to herself. And that was priceless.

Back at the cottage, Vittoria shooed Liam and Giorgio into the enclosed back garden while she cooked dinner.

'The princess is nothing like her sister, is she?' Liam said. 'So quiet and controlled. I guess it goes with her job.'

The security detail nodded. 'It will be good for her to have this break. She never takes time off.'

'Does she really have to marry whoever her family says she has to marry?'

Giorgio shrugged.

'What a waste,' Liam said softly. 'She de-serves someone who understands her, makes some space around her and makes her feel special.'

Giorgio's raised eyebrow spoke volumes.

'Don't worry. I know I can't be that man. I don't have blue blood and her family would never accept me,' Liam said. 'I'm not going to do anything inappropriate.' He really hoped the security detail didn't have a clue about that kiss last night. 'And I won't do anything to hurt her.'

'Good,' Giorgio said. 'Technically, she's my boss, but she feels like my little sister.'

'I have a little sister,' Liam reminded Giorgio, 'so I know exactly where you're coming from. You want to wrap them in cotton wool and save them from the harshest bits of the world. Though that isn't healthy, either. They need to learn to fly. And sometimes it's hard to find the middle way.'

'Very true,' Giorgio said.

'So what's he like? The guy her family want her to marry?'

Giorgio shrugged. 'It's not my place to judge.'

'OK. If she really was your little sister, would you be happy for her to marry him?'

'I'd want my little sister to marry someone who loved her for herself,' Giorgio said diplomatically. 'But the princess lives in a different world. One where people have expectations of her. Where everyone watches everything she says and does.'

A world where Liam knew he'd never fit in. And he heeded the warning. He wouldn't do anything to make Vittoria's life harder. 'I'll go grab us a drink from the fridge,' he said.

When he went into the kitchen, Vittoria was humming along to a pop song on the radio, making gnocchi. She seemed completely unaware of Liam's presence as he watched her; and she looked so cute, so relaxed, that he couldn't resist taking a couple of snaps on his phone.

A portrait of a princess; a portrait of her relaxing, doing something she enjoyed.

That was the thing missing from the formal portraits he'd taken, he realised. Happiness. In the formal ones, she'd been shouldering a weight. Here, she was free.

He wasn't going to break the moment for her; he quietly got two cans of drink from the fridge and went back into the garden.

Vittoria had already made the pesto while the potatoes were boiling. She enjoyed the task of making the gnocchi: sieving the cooked potatoes, cutting the flour in with a blunt knife and then kneading the dough with her hands. She'd forgotten how relaxing it could be, shaping the dough into the little balls and then flipping it along the tines of a fork to get

through. Particularly because it was specific, so it felt genuine rather than flattery. 'Thank you.'

'So what's the plan for tomorrow?' Giorgio asked.

'If it's dry we could go and look for bluebells,' Liam said. 'There are some bits of really ancient woodland here, and there's nothing more gorgeous than a bluebell carpet. The best time to visit is mid-morning, when you get all this soft, dappled light.'

'It sounds as if you've done a shoot in a bluebell wood before,' Vittoria said.

'I have. And among snowdrops, and in a poppy field.' He paused. 'You'd look spectacular in a poppy field. Very Monet.'

Was he seeing her with an artist's eye, or a man's?

She damped the thought down. They'd agreed that yesterday's kiss should be forgotten. The problem was, she couldn't forget it. It kept sliding back into her head, and even thinking about it made her mouth tingle.

Liam and Giorgio insisted on doing the washing up, and Giorgio made coffee.

'I'll sort out those photos for you,' Liam said, and downloaded the photographs from his phone and camera to his laptop at the kitchen table. 'Feel free to have a look,' he said when he'd finished. 'Let me know which ones you'd like, and I'll forward them to you.'

Their selfies on the boat with Giorgio looked as if they were just like all the other holiday-makers having fun. Vittoria chose one, plus the ones she'd taken of the seals, and he sent them to her phone.

Part of her wanted to ask for a copy of the portrait he'd taken in the palace library—that last, very private shot. But she knew she'd only brood over it, and it was pointless wishing for something she couldn't have. 'Thanks for sorting this out for me,' she said instead, and set out to compose a bright text to Izzy to go with the photographs.

CHAPTER FIVE

On Thursday morning, Liam drove them to a bluebell wood.

'I've never seen a bluebell carpet in real life. Not even when I lived in London,' Vittoria said as he parked the car.

'Really? There are loads of bluebells in Richmond Park and Highgate Woods. They were my mum's favourite flower. We used to go and see them every spring.' He smiled. 'After Mum died, I used to take Saoirse to see them and then we'd go for hot chocolate afterwards.'

'A way of remembering your mum?' she guessed.

He nodded. 'I wanted Saoirse to be able to remember her. And I thought a sight and a smell might help anchor it for her, as it does for me.'

It was a bit like the way Vittoria remembered walking with her dad through the palace rose garden and thought of him every time she smelled roses. Maybe she should share that with Izzy, to help her to remember their dad. 'I guess I was too busy studying and trying to learn some diplomatic duties to look for bluebells,' she said.

He frowned. 'Don't you have bluebells in San Rocello—or mainland Italy?'

'We have *giacinto di bosco*, yes, but they're not quite the same as English bluebells.'

He nodded. 'Dad taught me that English bluebells had narrower bells than European ones, and only on one side of the stem.'

It was the first time Liam had talked about his father to Vittoria, though she remembered him saying that his father had died when Saoirse was very small and he wasn't quite in double figures.

'Your father liked flowers?' she asked.

'He was a horticulturalist. He worked at Kew,' Liam explained.

'So you know a lot about plants?'

'Not that much,' he said, 'but we had an amazing garden at our old house. Mum kept it up after Dad died—he'd planted it so there would be colour all year round. Obviously at my flat now there's only the patio, and it's not fair to expect Saoirse to spend a lot of time on the plants if I'm away, so I just have stuff in pots that don't need a lot of attention. Though it's a shame. I want to keep Dad's memory alive, too.'

'Do you miss him?' The question was out before she could stop it.

'Yes. I guess you must feel the same about your dad. Wishing he could see you all grown up, wondering if you've grown into the person he thought you'd be. If he'd approve of your choices, your actions.'

She looked at him. 'Obviously I didn't know your dad—but I'm beginning to know you, and I think any parent would be proud to have a son like you. Someone who cares, who's made a huge difference to his little sister's life.'

There was a slash of colour in his cheeks. 'Thank you. And I think any dad would be proud of the woman I'm getting to know— someone who thinks, who notices details. Someone who's going to make a fair and balanced ruler.'

She inclined her head in acknowledgement. 'Thank you. Though I wasn't fishing for a compliment.'

'I didn't think you were. I wasn't, either. But it's hard growing up without a parent.' For a moment, his expression was bleak.

On impulse, she took his hand and squeezed it. 'Harder for you—at least I still have my mother. Even if she does drive me a bit crazy.'

'Mum used to wrap us both in cotton wool after Dad died,' Liam said. 'It was only when one of her friends had a quiet word with her about smothering us that she made an effort to be—well, more relaxed.'

Her own mother was definitely overprotective, Vittoria thought. Though she didn't have friends who would nudge her to be less smothering; if anything, Vittoria's grandmother encouraged her to be overprotective of both her daughters and the monarchy.

Then she realised she was still holding Liam's hand. Not the best idea, she reminded herself. 'My dad liked flowers, too,' she said, gently disentangling her fingers from his. 'I used to love walking in the palace rose garden with him. I still walk there, sometimes, because it makes me feel close to him.'

'I get that,' he said softly. 'And it's not just the sight, is it? It's the scent. The best rose garden I've ever seen is up on the north-east coast at Alnwick. I did a photo shoot there for a Sunday supplement and it was like breathing roses as you walked round. The scent was unbelievable.'

And then he stopped. 'Here's your bluebell carpet,' he said softly.

She hadn't really been paying attention to their surroundings as they walked; she'd been focused on him.

And there it was. A haze of blue underneath

the trees in the dappled sunlight, as far as the eye could see. The scent in the air was delicate, a kind of green floral. Vittoria closed her eyes for a moment to breathe it in, and knew this scent would always remind her of a late spring English morning—a morning spent with Liam.

They walked in silence; she was spellbound by the sheer beauty of the flowers, and took several snaps on her phone. Liam had his compact camera in his pocket and persuaded her to sit on a fallen tree and pose for pictures. 'I'm taking these for Izzy,' he said, and was very precise in his instructions for each pose.

Again, she saw the artist at work—and she liked what she saw. He was focused, intense, and she loved the sheer energy as he paced about, looked at her, changed his own position anywhere from being on tiptoe to squatting down, directed her to move her position or her head a little bit to get the precise angle he wanted, then took another shot.

He made her laugh when he asked her for what he called the classic female shots—one with her arms raised and her eyes closed and her head tilted back as if looking at the sky between the treetops; one with her holding one hand out towards him; one with her leaning against a tree trunk. It was surprisingly fun; she hadn't expected to enjoy this so much.

'Can I take a picture of you?' she asked, when he'd finished.

He looked slightly surprised, then nodded and handed over the camera. 'Sure.'

'So I assume there are rules for portrait photography?'

He smiled. 'A few. Though you don't always have to stick to the rules. You can break them—but it's better if you know *why* you're breaking them.'

He wasn't just talking about photography, was he? Her pulse leapt. 'Uh-huh,' she said, trying to sound calm and collected. Except she didn't feel calm or collected. She wanted him to kiss her again. And that wasn't fair.

With an effort, she said, 'Tell me the rules.' And then maybe she'd remember her personal rules, too.

'OK. With women, it's all about the curves; with men, it's about angles, so you're looking for a V shape with broad shoulders and a narrow waist. You're looking for a strong jaw, the eyes slightly squinting, and his head tilted away from the camera—but not too far, or he'll look arrogant and aggressive.'

She'd never thought about that before.

'Do you want me to face you full on or look away?' he asked.

'What's the best one?'

'That's your choice, because you're the one taking the portrait and telling the story,' he said. 'But even if it's face-on, you'd want your subject to turn very slightly so the nose is off-centre. That gives more shape and definition to the face.'

Liam had a beautiful nose. A beautiful face, she thought. And a mouth she desperately wanted to run her forefinger along and kiss again. She damped down the feelings. Not here, not now. 'Turn your face slightly to the left,' she directed, and he did so.

Funny, seeing him through the lens made her look at him differently. Made her focus on the little details. Everything from the corn-flower-blue of his eyes, to the length of his eyelashes, to the tiny grooves at the corners of his mouth which told her he smiled often.

'Next, decide what kind of light you want. It's up to you whether you want to use a flash, but consider that if the light source is from the same angle as the camera it'll flatten my features, because there aren't any shadows.'

She liked the way he explained things so clearly.

'Keep the composition simple. And check the background.' He smiled. 'In a forest, you don't want a tree trunk growing out of your subject's head or a branch growing out of an ear.'

'Got it.' She looked at the screen on the back of the camera. 'Right now, there's a tree growing out of your head. So I ask you to move, right?'

'Yes. And if I'm not looking straight at the camera, don't crop in too tightly. It's a better composition if you have some "lead room"—that's the space in a photo, between the subject and the edges of the picture. You need that to be in front of me, in the same direction as I'm looking. If the space is behind me, it makes your audience frustrated because there's all this empty space doing nothing, and they want to know what I'm looking at.'

'But if there's empty space in front of you, they still won't actually know what you're looking at,' she pointed out.

'True, but it means *I'm* the focus of the photograph—not, say, my ear,' he explained.

He talked her through a few more of the rules, and she took several shots in between each one, making him change his pose accordingly. Each picture was better than the previous one, because he'd taught her a little more. And it surprised her to realise that she was feeling more confident in her own abilities—more grounded. Not just in the skills he'd taught her this morning, but everything; he'd made her focus on her ability to see things, to plan and make decisions. Things that applied to more than taking a photograph.

Right at that moment, she felt strong: capable of doing anything. Because he was beside her? Or was he simply bringing out something that was already there? She'd been following so many rules for so long, she wasn't entirely sure. Maybe his own confidence in his skills— a confidence she found compelling—was rubbing off on her.

'So the poses you made me do... Are there male equivalents?'

'Yes. Though any pose can be gender-swapped. It depends on what you want to say with the picture,' he said. 'If I assume the pose, you tell me whether you need me to move, and if so how.'

And she loved every second of it. Seeing him put his right hand up to his chin, his thumb to the side and his index finger across his lips as if he was telling her this was a secret, a glint of mischief in his eyes. Standing almost side-on with his arms folded. Turning up the collar on his jacket, one hand on each lapel. Taking off his jacket and holding it over his shoulder with one finger, the other hand casually in his pocket. Leaning against a tree, with the leg closest to her bent up and his foot against the trunk.

It showed how strong his thighs were. And all of a sudden, she couldn't breathe. She could imagine him in a very different pose. On a hot summer night, when she'd woken and left their bed to get a cool drink… Naked, face down on a wide bed, with a sheet carelessly thrown across his lower body and showing how strong his back was, how perfect his musculature.

Heat prickled all the way through her.

'Done?' he asked.

Her mouth felt as if it had stuck to the roof of her mouth. Was this how he saw his models? Was this how he'd seen *her* when he'd asked her to pose for him?

'Vittoria? Are you OK?' There was a note of concern in his voice which snagged her attention away from the images in her head.

'Yes. Sorry. Wool-gathering.' She really hoped her thoughts hadn't shown in her face.

'Can I see the shots?'

She nodded mutely and gave his camera back.

He switched it to playback mode and scrolled through the shots. 'I can definitely see progress,' he said. 'You pay attention and you pick things up quickly. San Rocello's going to be lucky to have you in charge.'

The compliment warmed her all the way through. Particularly because she could tell it was sincere. She was used to people flattering her in the hope that she would give them influence or a business deal, but Liam didn't want anything from her.

But, oh, she was going to have to get those other images out of her head.

Because it couldn't happen. It couldn't last. And a fling with him—even if a future queen could abandon caution to the wind and have a mad fling—wouldn't be enough for her.

They strolled back to the car park, chatting easily, and he drove them further round the coast. They stopped to pick up sandwiches and takeaway coffee from a deli-café—he'd brought reusable mugs from the cottage—and then headed along a walkway at the edge of a pine forest.

'This one's gorgeous. It's been used as a film set quite a few times,' he said.

There were no beach huts here, and no cliffs. Just pine trees, a wide expanse of sand and an area that seemed to be covered in tiny flowers.

'It's a saltwater lagoon,' he said. 'When the tide comes in, it's covered.'

They walked along the beach together, with Giorgio as always giving them enough space to talk privately yet staying near enough to be there immediately if he was needed.

'I've been thinking. You said earlier you

want to be best portrait photographer of your generation, but aren't you that already?' she asked.

'I have a good reputation,' he said, 'but I think you can always learn more in your chosen field and do better. And I'm not where I want to be, yet.'

'So you're driven.'

'Yes,' he said, 'but I'm the one who makes the decisions on who's doing the driving.' He looked at her, his blue eyes thoughtful. 'You're just as driven as I am—but is being queen what you'd choose?'

'That's irrelevant,' she said. 'I always knew I'd be the queen some day because I'm the oldest child. If my father had lived, I would've taken over from him instead of from my grandfather.' Though she would've had more of a breathing space before the coronation. Right now, the end of the year felt very close indeed. Her last summer of freedom wasn't stretching out before her; it was going to vanish in the blink of an eye.

'If you weren't a princess—if you could do anything in the world—what would you do?' he asked.

'I don't honestly know,' she said. Because she deliberately hadn't let herself think about it. What was the point of wondering, when your path in life was already mapped out for you?

'I guess you never had the freedom to choose,' he said softly.

'No.' It hadn't mattered before, and she couldn't let it matter now. 'You didn't exactly have much freedom of choice, either,' she pointed out.

'True, but I don't think I missed out—maybe I missed out on having a social life at university, but since Saoirse turned eighteen I've been able to pretty much please myself with what I do and where I go. I know she won't do anything stupid like have a party and invite the kind of people who'd trash the flat.' He shrugged. 'I guess we both had to grow up fast.'

Vittoria rather thought he meant the two of them, rather than himself and his sister. 'It must've been tough, though, being a parent figure when you were so young yourself.'

'I had people I could ask for advice if I needed it. Patty, my old photography tutor, was so kind,' he said. 'But I guess I was lucky. Saoirse was in with a good crowd. It could've been much tougher.' He wrinkled his nose. 'My sister will always have a home with me, whenever she needs it. Just as I'm guessing you'd always find space for Izzy.'

'Yes. Of course I would.'

'But it's kind of put me off the idea of being a parent in the future. Been there, done that— I'll never regret putting her first, ever, but...' He blew out a breath. 'In the early days, every girlfriend I had seemed to end up resenting her. Probably my fault for picking the wrong kind of girl; they wanted to go to parties, and they got fed up when I couldn't find a baby-sitter.'

'She doesn't need a babysitter now.'

'No—but my career takes me away a lot. I have to go where my subject is. I can't expect them to come to me.'

'Why not?'

He smiled. 'Well, you were my last subject. Where would you say was the most appropriate place for the shoot—some random location in London, or the palace?'

'Point taken. But surely your girlfriends don't mind you travelling? Surely they like the chance to go with you?'

'It's not the travelling. It's the fact that my career comes first. If they came with me, I wouldn't be able to go and do touristy stuff with them because I'd be going there to work, not for a holiday. And I'm tired of being asked to choose,' he said. 'My family or my girlfriend; my career or my girlfriend.' He shrugged.

'Right now, I'm happily single—and I plan to stay that way. I want the freedom to follow my dream, to be the best photographer I can be. And if that means giving up on relationships, that's fine by me.'

He'd made his position very, very clear; he was single, and planning to stay that way.

Not that it was any of her business. And not that she was in a position to start a relationship with someone her family would definitely disapprove of. She knew her grandfather had liked Liam—but that was purely as an artist and a businessman. A potential partner for his eldest granddaughter was a very different matter. Plus, she'd learned from Rufus that having a non-royal background was the biggest hurdle to any relationship with a commoner. If anyone could overcome it, she thought Liam might be that man; from what she'd seen of him, he was bright, he paid attention to the small things, and he understood the struggle of responsibility. But he'd just made it clear he wasn't interested in a relationship.

This *Roman Holiday* thing was turning out to be a double-edged sword. On the one hand, it had given her a breathing space she'd desperately needed; on the other, it had given her space to dream of things that just weren't going to be possible in her real life. Right now,

she actually dreaded going back. She didn't
want to follow all the old rules any more. She
wanted to make new rules, ones that might
move life at the palace onto a more modern
footing. But was she strong enough to do that
on her own?

She concentrated on looking for pretty shells
and walking at the edge of the sea.

Today was the last day.

Tomorrow she'd be going back to the real
world. To the airport. To San Rocello. She
wouldn't be Vicky the tourist, walking barefoot on a beach, any more; she'd be Princess
Vittoria, wearing the perfect business suit and
high heels. And the weight that had lightened
on her first day here settled right back in the
centre of her shoulders.

She didn't say much for the rest of the afternoon; and Liam, clearly realising that she
didn't want to talk, didn't push her. She managed to make small talk during dinner at a
local foodie pub, chatting about how delicious the locally made goat's cheese was, and
the seafood risotto. Things that didn't really
matter.

And then they were back at the cottage,
where Giorgio pleaded a headache and a need
for an early night.

Was that what she should do? Borrow a book

from the shelves in the living room and have an early night, too?

But Liam said quietly, 'It's your last night. It's a nice evening; come and sit in the garden with a glass of wine.'

The wine was crisp, dry and perfectly chilled. Liam had put cushions on two wrought-iron chairs, and they sat side by side, looking up at the stars.

'Penny for them?' he asked.

She had intended to be polite and not admit to what was really going on in her head, but something in his eyes made her tell the truth. 'I've enjoyed my time here. It's really helped recharge me. Izzy's right about the palace making me feel stifled. But I know I have to go back to San Rocello.' And do her duty. Which she'd already shirked for four whole days.

Either she'd spoken aloud or he was seriously good at working out what people were thinking, because he asked, 'Do you really have to get married to this guy your family's chosen for you?'

'José?' She sighed. 'Probably. Or someone like him.'

'I understand that you have to marry someone from a royal background,' he said, 'but can't you choose him yourself?'

'Sometimes I wonder—' She stopped and screwed up her nose. 'Forget I said that.'

He looked at her. 'Sometimes it helps to think out loud and bounce ideas off people.'

If she talked to anyone about this, it should be Izzy. But she hadn't wanted to burden her sister, especially so close to Izzy's Finals.

'If it helps,' he said, 'I promise it won't go any further than me.'

She thought about it. Given how much time Izzy had spent at his flat over the last three years, he would know a lot about her sister's life. If he'd wanted to sell a story to the press, he'd had plenty of opportunities, and he definitely had the contacts. But he'd done nothing of the kind.

She could trust him.

If she chose.

'I feel disloyal even thinking this,' she said. 'I know what my family expects from me. I'm going to be queen. I need to marry, produce an heir and a spare, and bring up those children so they'll be able to do their own duty well, when it's their time. And of course I'll do my duty, just as my father would've done if he'd still been alive—just as my grandfather has done.'

'But would it be different if your dad hadn't died?' he asked. 'Obviously you'd still eventually be queen, but would you have been able to choose your own husband?'

'I don't know,' she admitted. 'I think maybe my dad would've wanted me to find someone I loved—someone who loved me.'

'So who's putting the pressure on you to marry someone you don't love? Your grandfather?'

She shook her head. 'My mum and my grandmother. Nonna's very traditional—and I think when my dad died my mum found it hard to cope. She's pretty much followed my grandmother's lead in everything since then, wrapping me up in cotton wool and…' She shook her head. 'I love my mother. But sometimes I wish she'd lighten up. I wish she'd find another partner—not because it would take the pressure off me, but because I worry that she's lonely.'

Liam took her hand and squeezed it. 'As lonely as *you* are?'

'If so much as a single word of this gets back to Izzy, you're toast,' she warned, scowling at him.

'It won't,' he reassured her. 'Not because I'm scared of you, but because I know how you feel. I try not to let Saoirse know if I'm out of sorts about something, too.'

'Thank you.' She sighed. 'Being at the palace can be a bit isolating. I've got my mum, and my grandparents, and that's it. My local friends have all moved away, my uni friends are scattered across the globe, and—oh, this is turning into such a pity party.' She grimaced. 'And that's not who I am.'

'Of course it isn't. You're bright, you're independent, and you're about to shoulder a really heavy responsibility. I mean, don't most monarchs accede the throne when they're fifty or so?' he asked.

'I guess.'

'It's a lot of pressure. And I agree with you: it's not a good idea to get married to someone you don't love and who doesn't love you. You're going to have enough on your plate. Talk to your grandfather. Tell him you need more time to find the right partner. Tell them you'd like to choose your own husband. You're going to be queen, so surely you get to make some of the rules?'

'And if they all say no?'

'Negotiate,' he said. 'To do a job well, you need to be happy in that job. And you're not going to be happy shackled to someone who doesn't understand you. As the queen, you need a consort you can rely on. Someone you can talk to. Someone with a bit of common sense. Someone who understands your heart.'

She inclined her head. 'Sadly, consorts

don't quite come to order.' She looked up at the stars in the sky. 'Do you ever wonder if there's more?'

'To the universe? Maybe. You?'

'I...' She pushed the longing back down. 'No.'

'Or did you mean more than life in a gold-fish bowl?' he asked gently.

How could he see through her like that? Was her public mask slipping? Would other people see it, too? Or was it because Liam had a connection with her that he could tell what was going on in her head?

'What you asked me among the bluebells this morning—if I could do anything I wanted, what would it be? I've been thinking about it all day and I still don't have an answer.'

He didn't push her.

And finally, she admitted, 'Sometimes I'm not sure who I am, deep down.'

'When I take a portrait,' he said, 'it shows me who someone is. I get them to talk to me. Tell me their hopes, their dreams. Sometimes it's obvious they're not telling me what they really feel, so I ask questions from completely left field. Stupid things, like those internet quizzes Saoirse and Izzy love about what sort of cookie you are. Or I ask them to read something, or tell me a joke—and then, once they open up to me, I can take a portrait of who they are.'

She remembered her own photo shoot with him. 'You asked me to read you my favourite poem.'

He inclined his head. 'Shakespeare's *Sonnet 130*. And that told me a lot about you. Vittoria, I know you have a duty, but it doesn't make sense to marry someone you don't love.'

She had no choice. She had to marry someone who understood protocol and the demands of a royal lifestyle. Love on its own wasn't enough, or Rufus wouldn't have backed away from her.

Liam took his phone from his pocket and tapped into a website.

'These are the photographs I took for your grandfather. Your official portrait,' he said. 'Look at her from the outside. Pretend this is a stranger, not you. Can you see what I see? A woman who's proud of the traditions she comes from. A princess. Someone cool, calm and collected. Reliable in a crisis. Prepared to do the best for her people.'

Where was he going with this?

'Unofficially…' He showed her the photographs he'd taken when she hadn't even been aware of him using his phone: of her on the beach, of her making the gnocchi. When she'd been relaxed. When she'd felt happy.

'And this.' The photographs they'd taken in the bluebell wood that morning, when she'd been laughing and smiling and intrigued by him. When she'd done the poses she'd thought at the time were a bit ridiculous, but had gone along with them because she could see he was having fun, and she'd enjoyed it too.

'Maybe I'm presuming things, but as a photographer I'm used to looking past the trappings and seeing who someone really is. I think these photographs show the real you,' he said, 'the one that people don't see. A woman who's usually reserved, but here you're the woman behind the tiara. Laughing. Open. Beautiful. Izzy says you're like sunshine when you smile. And you are.'

She'd never heard her little sister say that about her, and it brought a lump to her throat.

And then he flicked over to the photograph he'd taken of her in the library.

'*This* is you,' he said, his voice cracking. 'The you I saw. The you I kissed on the beach. The you I wanted to kiss among the bluebells this morning, when you were pretending to be me and bossing me about.' He paused. 'The you I want to kiss now, even though I know it's unfair of me because you have to go back to San Rocello and you have duties to fulfil. The you I want to kiss now, even though I'm not looking for a relationship—and even if I was, I know there isn't a snowflake's chance in hell of things working out between us.'

She knew he was right.

She could be sensible Princess Vittoria, agree with him there wasn't a hope for them, and walk away.

Or she could be herself. The woman who wanted him to kiss her. Who wanted to kiss him back. Who wanted more.

Just for tonight…

She'd never felt such a strong compulsion before. Longing. It wasn't just about sex—though there was definitely desire there—it was about *connection*.

Tentatively, she stretched out a hand and stroked his cheek.

He slid his hand over hers, then turned his head so he could drop a kiss into her palm. Then he gently drew her hand away and kissed her in the garden under the stars, his mouth warm and sweet and enticing.

This time, they had birdsong rather than the swish of the waves for background noise.

This time, there wasn't anyone to interrupt them with an ill-timed shout.

It was just the two of them, the stars and the nightingales. It felt as if rainbows were filling her head, and she'd never wanted anyone as much as she'd wanted this man.

She broke the kiss. 'Liam.'

He sighed. 'Vittoria. I'm sorry. I know I overstepped the line.'

'No. I wanted you to kiss me.' She took a deep breath, thinking about the moment in the bluebell wood when she'd had that vision of him naked and in her bed. When desire had been so strong, it had stopped up her words. 'I want more than kissing. I want you.'

His cornflower-blue eyes were almost indigo. 'I want you, too. But we can't do this. It's going to hurt too many people.'

She shook her head. 'There's nobody to hurt. I'm single. You are, too.'

'But your family's arranging a marriage.'

To someone she didn't love. Someone who didn't make her pulse beat a tattoo, the way it was beating right now. And maybe Liam had given her enough to think about tonight. Maybe she didn't have to marry someone so fast. Maybe she could take her time and choose her consort wisely.

She took a deep breath. 'I'll do my duty, when the time comes. But this is now. Time for me. My *Roman Holiday*, as Izzy calls it. You, me, no strings.' A fling she knew a queen-to-be couldn't have; but Liam had said earlier that you could break the rules, as long as you knew why.

She knew why she wanted to break the rules tonight.

She wanted him.

Wanted him more than she'd ever wanted anyone in her life.

He brushed his mouth against hers. 'Just so you know, I don't sleep around.'

'Neither do I.' She took another deep breath. 'But I can't get you out of my head, Liam. I haven't been able to stop thinking about you since that moment in the library. I thought you were going to kiss me, then.'

'I almost did,' he admitted.

'I wish you had.'

He shook his head. 'I never mix work and my personal life. And that photo shoot was work.'

'That last picture in the library wasn't,' she said. 'You didn't take that for my grandfather, or even for Izzy, or she would've shown me.'

'No. I admit, I took it for me. Because you're captivating,' he said. 'You're the most beautiful woman I've ever met, but it's not just the way you look. It's *you*. The way you make me feel. I can't stop thinking about you, either. But we don't have a future. I have my career to think of and you have your duty. I'd never fit into your world, and you can't fit into mine.

I wouldn't ask you to choose between me and your duty because it wouldn't be fair.'

'I know.' She sighed. 'And I wish things were different.'

'So do I. But they're not. We need to be sensible.'

She stared at him. 'How can I be sensible when you're still touching me?'

Before he could pull his hand away from her cheek, she twisted her head to the side, just as he'd done to her, and pressed a kiss into his palm.

He sucked in a breath. 'What do we do about this, Vittoria?'

She was glad he hadn't called her by that ridiculous borrowed name. He saw her for who she was. Vittoria. Not the princess, but the woman. She looked him straight in the eye. 'We might not be able to have for ever—but we can have tonight. A moment out of time.'

There was a deep slash of colour across his cheeks as he thought about what she'd just said and clearly came to the right conclusion.

'Do you have a condom?' she asked.

He inclined his head.

'Then what I want,' she said, just in case it wasn't clear enough, 'is to spend tonight with you. To make love with you. To wake in your arms.'

'And Giorgio?'

'He wouldn't come into my room. He'd knock and maybe talk to me through my door, but he wouldn't come in—not unless he had reason to think I was in danger.' In a way, she was in danger. In danger of losing her heart to Liam. When she was with him, she didn't feel stifled under the weight of duty. She was herself.

But she'd made the terms of this clear. It was just for tonight. A moment out of their real lives, for both of them. One night with no future. And, even though it scared her that doing this might mean that no man would ever match up to him and she'd have to settle for second best, that was still better than never being with him at all.

'Your room?' he asked softly.

'That's actually your room, isn't it?'

'Yes.' He stole a kiss. 'Are you telling me you were thinking about that? About me sleeping in your bed?'

She felt the colour flood into her cheeks. 'Yes.'

He stole another kiss. 'I did the same.'

'And I thought of you, this morning,' she whispered. 'I imagined taking a photograph of you asleep. In my bed. Face down, with a sheet thrown casually over you, and your back…' Her mouth dried.

'I don't do nudes, even arty ones,' he said. 'But that's how I'd want to photograph you, too. Your hair loose and tumbled over my pillow, a sheet drawn up with one hand, looking all shy and adorable.'

'Take me to bed, Liam,' she said.

He didn't need a second urging, though he did pause long enough in the kitchen to kiss her and then to lock the back door. 'Because, once I'm in bed with you,' he said, his voice low and husky, 'I don't want to have to leave until the morning.'

'That works for me.'

And a delicious shiver of excitement rippled down her spine when he picked her up in the living room and carried her up two flights of stairs to her room.

'Caveman,' she teased.

'Better believe it,' he teased back, and held her close as he set her back on her feet, leaving her in no doubt about how much he wanted her.

And then he kissed her again, and she stopped thinking about anything at all.

CHAPTER SIX

THE NEXT MORNING, Vittoria was woken by the dawn light filtering through the curtains, even though they were lined. She lay on her side in the wide bed, with Liam curled protectively round her, his arm wrapped round her and drawing her close to his body.

He'd been a gentle but intense lover, exploring and discovering where she liked being kissed or touched, what made her catch her breath with desire.

Last night had been a revelation.

Nobody, even Rufus, had ever made her feel like this.

But she knew Liam was right. This thing between them didn't stand a chance of working out. Her background was what had made Rufus break up with her all those years ago. If you weren't from that kind of background, life in a royal family would be tough to cope with. Even if you were used to fame and dealing with the media in a different arena, it wasn't the same as living in a goldfish bowl. Plus, Liam had explicitly told her that he wasn't looking for a relationship. His career came first.

She lay there for a few precious minutes, savouring the feel of his skin against hers and wishing things could be different. That there was a way for them to be together. But, whatever way she looked at it, she couldn't find a solution.

Eventually she felt him stir and draw her closer. His breathing changed, signalling to her that he'd woken. When his lips grazed her shoulder, she turned round to face him.

He kissed the tip of her nose. 'Good morning.'

'Good morning.' And it was more than good, waking in his arms.

'I need to go back to my own room,' he said.

Before Giorgio realised what had happened. Yeah. She knew. 'I wish…' Though it was pointless saying it out loud; it would only make her feel miserable, because things *couldn't* be different.

'Me, too.' He kissed her one last time. 'You know your favourite poem? Just for the record, my mistress' eyes are nothing like the sun. They're this amazing, *amazing* blue. Until yesterday, I would've said violet blue—but, actually, they're the shade of a newly unfurled English bluebell. I really wish I'd asked you to remove those contact lenses yesterday, so I could've taken a proper shot to showcase your eyes.'

The compliment made her feel warm all over. Nobody had ever said something like that to her. Liam saw her with an artist's eye— the woman, not the princess. And she loved the fact he actually quoted poetry. Particularly as he knew her favourite poem; again, it made her feel that he understood what made her tick.

It was on the tip of her tongue to suggest they went back to London this morning via the bluebell wood, but she knew it would be a mistake. Yesterday was yesterday. Last night was last night. A one-off. Never to be repeated.

He twirled one unruly curl round his finger. 'And this. I knew you'd look cute with your hair all messy in the morning.' He grinned. 'Shakespeare's black wires, I think.'

This was goodbye. So she let herself twine her fingers through his hair. 'You look cute and messy this morning, too. And your eyes are the same blue as cornflowers.' She stroked his cheek. 'I'd be worried if *this* was a damask red rose, though.'

'Hard-drinking photographer, face pasty

white from a nocturnal partying lifestyle and starting to get broken veins in my face from all the alcohol,' he said.

Which made her laugh. From what she'd seen, Liam MacCarthy worked hard rather than drank hard. He didn't give her the impression that he was a party animal—if anything, she rather thought he'd find them dull—and during this week he'd been up early rather than staying awake all night and sleeping all day. 'Yeah.'

'Coral.' He rubbed the pad of his thumb along her lower lip. 'I always thought that was an orangey colour. Your mouth is more rose-coloured. By which I mean pink.'

She really didn't want the day to start. She definitely didn't want him to leave her bed.

But she had a plane to catch, and he had a life to get back to.

Dragging out their parting would only make both of them miserable. Better to cut it short now.

'I'm not very good at goodbyes,' she said.

'Me, neither.' He paused. 'So let's say good-bye now. When I drop you off at Izzy's place—as Vicky—I won't see you again before you leave for San Rocello.'

'I know.' And how that made her ache.

'You and me—it can't work. Not in the real

world. You have responsibilities and I have my career.' His eyes were filled with regret.

'I know.' She took a deep breath. 'We probably won't see each other again.' They moved in different worlds. And anyway, she'd hate having to be a polite stranger with him, pretending that last night had never happened. It was pointless trying to cling on to something that didn't have a foundation, something that would just make them both miserable.

'The last few days—they were a moment out of time for both of us,' he agreed. 'Don't worry. I won't sell you out to the press.'

She stroked his face. 'I already knew that. I just wish…'

'…it could be different. So do I,' he said softly. 'But we both have to be sensible.'

Sometimes sex just wasn't enough. Right now, she wanted to remember the feel of Liam holding her, the shape of his body round hers, the touch of his skin. She held him tightly, without speaking. And he was holding her just as tightly, so she was pretty sure he felt the same way. Both of them wanting what they couldn't have, and neither of them able to see a solution that worked for both of them. She couldn't give up her job, and she knew it would break his heart to give up his. There was no middle ground, no compromise.

Finally, he kissed the top of her head. 'I'll see you downstairs for breakfast,' he said softly.

She knew she ought to say something witty. Make a joke. Even though right at the moment it felt as if her heart was cracking. 'Just as long as Giorgio's the one in charge of making the coffee,' she said lightly.

'Yes, ma'am.'

She knew he was teasing, but his words also put the official distance back between Princess Vittoria di Sarda of San Rocello and Liam MacCarthy. The royal and the commoner. The photographer and his subject.

After he'd gone she showered, changed into her borrowed wig and clothes and the contact lenses, packed, and stripped the bedding.

She kept everything light over a breakfast of toast, local lemon curd and coffee; Liam drove them back to London and dropped her and Giorgio at Izzy's flat. There were no photographers around to notice her, so her disguise wasn't really needed. But she damped down her longing for more time with Liam and enjoyed spending the rest of her time in London making a fuss of her little sister.

Once at Izzy's flat, she asked Giorgio to go to a bookshop for her to buy a copy of the new biography of Karsh. She wrote a brief message inside the flyleaf.

Liam. Thank you for everything. Vittoria.

She posted it on the way to the airport, and she was sitting on the plane back to San Rocello when she checked her email. There was one from Liam, sending her a link to his website and giving her an access code.

The web page made it very clear that this was a private portfolio, one which you could only log into if you had the access code. She typed in the code he'd given her, and as soon as she opened the gallery she realised that Liam had sent her all the photographs from her time with him in Norfolk—the ones he'd taken of her, and the ones she'd taken of him—as well as that very private one he'd taken of her in the palace library.

This felt like a message. Maybe she was just presuming things, but it felt as if this was his way of confirming to her what he'd promised earlier: that what had happened between them would stay private. The photographs, the closeness, the things she'd told him. And the fact he'd sent her that private photograph told her that she could trust him.

She studied the photographs carefully. He

was right; she did look carefree and happy. But the camera had also picked up something else, something she really hoped he hadn't seen for himself: that she'd lost her heart to him. Because the look on her face was definitely the look of someone in love. She looked all starry-eyed, even behind those ridiculous contact lenses. If she was honest with herself, that was exactly how she felt about him. She liked him as a person—his dependability, his strength, the way he noticed things. Physically, he made her heart beat faster just with a look or a smile. But it was more than simple liking or physical attraction. During those few days at the coast she'd fallen in love with him.

What was she going to do?

She and Liam had already agreed that things simply couldn't work out between them. They didn't have a future.

But she really couldn't accept an arranged marriage with José: a man she didn't love now and didn't think she ever would.

She knew she was expected to get married, for the sake of her duty—if nothing else, she needed to produce an heir—but she remembered what Liam had said about her needing a consort she could rely on. Someone she could talk to, who understood her. He'd advised her to talk to her family, explain that she needed more time. Negotiate.

To negotiate well, you needed to be clear on all your facts. She was going to approach this in the same way as she did all her other royal duties: with care and consideration. So she spent the rest of the flight reading San Rocello's constitution very closely, rather than mooning over photos of Liam MacCarthy.

By the time the plane touched down, she was smiling, armed with the facts she needed: certain clauses in the constitution were very explicit about the fact that the king or queen didn't have to be married before he or she could accede the throne.

And this gave her the confidence to stand up to the pressure.

Liam made another print of a photograph from the bluebell woods shoot, this time making a really tight crop.

Vittoria di Sarda was beautiful.

Beyond beautiful.

Even with the wrong hair and the wrong eyes, she captivated him. It was in the curve of her mouth, the tiny laughter lines beginning to fan out from the corners of her eyes, the way she tilted her head.

And how he wished he'd taken some shots

of her, this morning. When he'd been teasing her with her favourite poem, and she'd laughed up at him from the pillow.

The only images he had from that were in his mind's eye, and it wasn't enough. How long would it be before the images faded, before he forgot the feel of her skin against his and the scent of her hair?

He never usually let himself get that close to his girlfriends. Balancing his family and his job was hard enough; he'd found adding a relationship and all its demands into the mix led to feeling guilty that he wasn't focusing well enough on any area of his life.

And now he'd fallen for a woman who was completely out of his reach. He'd fallen for the woman with her cool, calm, collected carapace. He'd fallen even harder for the woman beneath that carapace: the woman who'd asked for an on-the-fly photography lesson and cheekily taken his portrait, the woman who'd walked barefoot at the edge of the sea with him.

The woman who'd kissed him underneath the stars.

'A rose by any other name would smell as sweet...'

The words bounced into his head. Forget the name. Vittoria was still a princess and always would be. But roses... He wanted to photograph her in a rose garden. He wanted to kiss her in a rose garden. He wanted to scatter rose petals on the crisp white sheets of a wide, wide bed and make love with her by the light of the moon.

And how weird was it that his aim of being the best portrait photographer of his generation suddenly felt so empty and pointless? The images weren't enough for him any more. He wanted something else: he wanted Vittoria. In his arms. Always.

'It's not going to happen,' he told himself out loud. 'So just snap out of it and get on with your work.'

'What do you mean, you're not going to marry José?' Princess Maria demanded, looking aghast at her eldest daughter.

'Exactly what I said, Mamma.' One good thing about learning to look composed in public, no matter how you felt inside, was that you could do it just as successfully in your private life. So Vittoria sipped her coffee casually, making it look as if she didn't have a care in the world. Inwardly, she was a churning mess.

'You know you have to get married before you accede the throne,' Queen Giulia, her grandmother, added.

'Mamma, Nonna—I love you both dearly

and I respect you,' Vittoria said quietly, 'but in this case I can't do what you ask of me. I don't want to marry someone I barely know and who has nothing in common with me other than his background. I want the time and space to choose who I marry, rather than rushing in. And I've read the constitution. Very thoroughly. There isn't actually a legal requirement for the monarch to be married.'

Maria's mouth tightened. 'I don't care what the constitution says. It's like Nonna says. Our people expect their ruler to be settled. So you need to get married and *show* them you're settled.'

'Mamma, they already know I'm settled. I'm not the sort to spend my life partying and gadding about. I've taken on more and more duties from Nonno every year, representing our country on numerous occasions, and I've done the job well.'

'But you need an heir,' Maria said.

'And a spare. I know. But there isn't a legal requirement for me to marry before I become queen, and it would be so much more sensible not to rush things. We need to find the right consort for the country—and for me.'

'I think there's more to this than meets the eye,' Maria said darkly. 'This secret getaway of yours—did you meet up with Rufus again? Is *that* what all this is about?'

'No. I haven't seen Rufus in years.' Looking back now, Vittoria was pretty sure that her mother and grandmother had tried to show Rufus that he'd never fit in to the palace. No wonder he'd backed away. It would take someone much stronger than Rufus to stand up to her family.

'Is there someone else?' Giulia asked.

Yes. Liam's face flashed into her head. Liam, in her bed, that last morning, teasing her with Shakespeare and then kissing her until they were both dizzy. 'No.' And it was the truth: Liam had made it very clear that he couldn't and wouldn't offer her for ever. She'd fallen for a man who was out of reach, so effectively there wasn't someone else. 'I'm simply saying that I'm ready to be queen but I'm not rushing into marriage. I want time to get to know my future husband and fall in love with him before I get married.'

Maria's mouth thinned. 'Marriages aren't about love.'

'I disagree. Marriage should be all about love,' Vittoria said.

'I know you loved Rufus, and he loved you—but he wouldn't have been able to cope with life as your consort,' Maria said, this time a little more gently. 'You need someone who's been brought up with this background, someone who won't buckle under the pressure. It's not an easy thing to do.'

'I need more than that,' Vittoria said. 'I need someone who loves me for me. Who sees me for who I am, underneath all the trappings of royalty.'

Someone like Liam MacCarthy.

'It doesn't happen like that for people like us,' Giulia said.

Vittoria looked at her grandmother, shocked. 'Are you saying you don't love Nonno?'

'Of course I love your grandfather. But I had to learn to love him,' Giulia said.

'Just as I learned to love your father, and just as you will learn to love José,' Maria added.

'With respect, Mamma and Nonna, I disagree. I know traditions are important to you both, but traditions should underpin a monarchy, not lock it into the past.' Vittoria lifted her chin. 'Society changes, and a monarchy needs to change with its people, so it stays relevant. I want our country to be at the forefront, not seen by the rest of the world as a place that can't move on.'

Her mother and grandmother frowned, but at least neither of them was trying to shout her down. This time, perhaps, they were listening to what she said.

'I worry about you, Rina.' The use of the pet name alerted Vittoria. 'I was so worried when I found out you'd taken this ridiculous secret break.'

Worry. That was the crux of it, Vittoria knew. Her father had died in a sailing accident—and Maria was clearly panicking that something might befall her eldest daughter in the same way. It was why she wrapped both her daughters in a suffocating mix of cotton wool and tradition.

'Mamma, I didn't take any reckless risks. I stayed well away from the edges of cliffs, and I didn't swim out of my depth or anywhere near a riptide. No water-skiing, no paragliding, nothing to worry about at all. I was perfectly safe. Giorgio was with me.' Something suddenly occurred to her. The last thing she wanted was for her security detail to get into trouble. 'It was my idea, so don't blame him, Mamma. He did his job perfectly, keeping me safe. And Nonno was fine about it.' Which was true. After a slightly uncomfortable interview, King Vittorio had come round to his grand-daughter's point of view.

'I know you think we wrap you in cotton wool,' Maria said. 'But we lost Francesco.'

* * *

'Thanks.' Liam took the parcel from the post-man. He hadn't ordered anything online, and he wasn't expecting anything. The address on the front was in handwriting he didn't recognise. Frowning, he looked at the back. There was a London postcode, but the surname didn't mean anything to him.

Still puzzled, he opened it to discover a hardback biography of his favourite photographer. There was nothing else in the parcel; he opened the flyleaf, and then he saw the inscription.

Liam. Thank you for everything. Vittoria.

It was a book he'd been meaning to order for himself. She must've remembered him saying how much he admired Karsh. Typical Vittoria, having perfect manners and sending her host a thank-you gift.

But in those six words there was definite finality.

She'd used someone else's surname when posting the book—he assumed either Giorgio or Pietro.

But it would be rude not to thank her for the gift, he told himself, ignoring the fact that part

'We couldn't bear losing you, too,' Giulia added. 'It was bad enough when you went to study in London. Every time we turned on the news and heard about an accident or a fire or some terrible thing happening, we worried.'

'And when nobody knew where you were, these last few days… We were frantic,' Maria said.

'Izzy knew,' Vittoria said gently. 'And I'm pretty sure Giorgio would have called Nonno if he thought I was taking too much of a risk.' She took a deep breath. 'I know you both love me—as I love you—and I understand that you worry about me. But I need to *live*. I can't be a good ruler if I feel stifled all the time. This isn't about disrespecting you, but we need to find a better compromise. One where you worry less and I breathe more.'

'So you refuse to marry José,' Maria said.

'I do,' Vittoria confirmed. 'Becoming queen will be hard. I need you both on my side, not fighting against me.'

'We just don't want you to make a mistake,' Giulia said. 'Rufus was a mistake.'

'Maybe if we'd supported him better, taught him how to deal with the royal lifestyle, it could have worked,' Vittoria said. 'I can't change the past. But I'm saying no to José.

I will discuss it with you—of course I will, because you're both important to me—but at the end of the day I need someone I can feel comfortable with. Someone I can trust.' Someone like Liam—though she knew that was too much to wish for. 'And, while you're thinking about that, I'll go and get some more coffee from the kitchen.'

'You're going to be the queen at the end of the year,' Maria said. 'The queen doesn't go to the kitchen on an errand.'

'Actually, Mamma, I think the queen *should* go to the kitchen on an errand, from time to time. The castle doesn't run itself. I have a responsibility to the staff here—to make sure they're properly supported in their jobs. Which I can't do if I don't have a clue what's going on or who any of them are, or what they do. A good leader understands a business from the bottom up—and nowadays a monarchy is equivalent to a business.' She lifted her chin. 'I'm not going to be a figurehead queen. I did my MBA in London, remember. I understand the challenges a business faces, and I've always intended to be a working queen. One who listens to her subjects and does her best for her people and her country.'

Maria was clearly about to say something, but Giulia placed a hand on her arm. 'Our girl

has a point, Maria. And we've always taught her to respect our staff—we cannot function well as a monarchy without them. Understanding what they do will deepen Rina's understanding of our people.'

Maria looked at her. 'You're not a little girl any more, Rina. You've grown up.'

Vittoria hadn't been a little girl for a long, long time. But it was good that her mother had finally noticed. 'I'll always be your daughter, Mamma,' she said gently. 'But, yes, I'm old enough to make my own decisions. Good ones. Ones I've thought through.'

Giulia's eyes filled with tears. 'Your father would have been so proud of you.'

'I hope so. And I hope I'll make you both proud of me, too. You've both taught me so much,' Vittoria said. 'But, please, call off the negotiations with José's family. It isn't fair to either of us.'

Maria and Giulia looked at her for a long, long moment.

Then Maria nodded. 'All right. We'll do it your way.'

Vittoria hugged them. 'Thank you for trusting me,' she said. 'And in future I'll try not to worry you.'

'And we,' Giulia said, 'will try not to make you feel so smothered.'

of him was jumping at the chance to contact her again.

He emailed her.

Thank you for the book. I'd been meaning to order a copy. Liam.

The reply came later in the day. Short, polite, but not inviting further conversation.

You're very welcome. Vittoria.

Time to leave it, he thought, and buried himself back into work.

'What's this in aid of?' Liam asked a few days later, eyeing the excellent coffee and wholemeal chicken salad sandwich that Saoirse had brought him, along with an apple.

'I'm just making sure you eat something nutritious. You've skipped dinner three times in the last week, so either you're forgetting to eat because you're so busy, or you're stuffing your face with fast food because you're hungry and it's quick. Even if you scoff junk for the rest of today, I'll know that, if you've eaten this, you'll have had two of your five portions a day. And that's probably better than any other day this week.'

Bless her. She was trying to look after him, the way he'd looked after her for years. He gave her a hug. 'Love you, Sursh.'

'Love you, too. But I really am worried about you, Liam. You're working crazy hours, even by your standards.' She pulled back slightly. 'Can you delegate anything to me, or maybe hire an assistant?'

'No.'

'Why not?'

Telling her the truth would mean admitting that he was trying to keep himself too busy to think about Vittoria. 'I'm fine. You know what my job's like, all peaks and troughs. I had a few days off recently, and now I'm making up for it.'

Her eyes narrowed. 'Did something happen while you were away?'

Yes. I fell in love with your best friend's sister and I don't know what to do about it, so I'm burying myself in work. 'No,' he fibbed.

She didn't look as if she believed him. 'You always take a gazillion pics when you go to Norfolk. You haven't shown me a single photograph, this time.'

He'd taken photographs. He just didn't want to show her, because they were a dead give-away and he wanted to protect Vittoria as well as himself. The princess all dreamy in the blue-bells; the princess relaxing by the sea and un-bending into a woman he wanted so much it was like a visceral ache. 'I was busy showing Izzy's sister round.' *And falling in love with her.* He pushed the thought away. He couldn't afford to fall in love with her. They didn't—couldn't—have a future.

'Vittoria's been acting weirdly, too. She's been really quiet with Izzy. And she tells Izzy *everything.*'

Liam knew that wasn't strictly true. Vittoria obviously hadn't told Izzy about their near-kiss at the palace, or Izzy would've told Saoirse. And Vittoria definitely wouldn't have told Izzy about their stolen night together. She'd also sworn him to secrecy about how lonely and isolated she felt at the palace, asking him to keep it from Izzy—to protect her little sister from the knowledge. But she'd shared it with *him*… 'She's probably just busy, catching up on all the stuff she didn't do when she had those unplanned days off over here.'

'I suppose so.' Saoirse shook her head. 'Something doesn't feel quite right, but I can't put my finger on it.'

Liam had no intention of explaining it to her. 'I honestly think you're worrying over noth-ing. But thank you for the sandwich.'

After his sister had left, he leaned back thoughtfully in his chair. So Vittoria was acting weirdly and being quiet with her sister. That was exactly the way Saoirse was complaining that he was behaving. So what did that mean? Was she missing him as much as he was missing her? Did she lie awake at night, wondering if there was some kind of middle way where she'd get to do her regal stuff, he'd get to follow his career dreams, and they could be together?

He had no idea.

They'd said it was goodbye. They both knew there was no point in dragging things out, trying to cling on to some form of friendship. Even when she'd sent him the book and he'd thanked her for it, there had been a tacit agreement that it was over.

But maybe it wasn't.

Maybe it was time to open up a conversation and find out how she felt.

And he was shocked to feel a weird flicker somewhere around the region of his ribcage. He couldn't quite put a name to it, but he thought it might be hope.

Talking without words.

It was what he did for a living: telling a story through a picture.

Maybe this was the way forward.

Later that day, he searched through his digital archive and fished out a shot of a rose that he'd taken during a shoot in a garden.

A single red rose.

How would the future Queen of San Rocello interpret his message? And, more importantly, was he fooling himself—or would she reply?

A picture of a rose. Without comment. There was definitely meaning in this, Vittoria knew. Liam wasn't the sort of man who'd send something at random. It was deliberate. A red rose. Was Liam referring to what she'd told him about walking in the palace gardens when the roses were in bloom, and feeling close to her dad? Was this his way of telling her he missed her?

She definitely missed him. In odd little moments during the day, when she found herself looking at the photographs she'd taken of him, and wished she was back under the stars with him. Or when she woke in the middle of the night and her bed felt much too wide, and she wished she was back in that little room overlooking the sea. It wasn't just loneliness; it was *his* company she missed. Waking in his arms and talking, as they had on that last morning. With him, she could be herself. And she missed that, too.

She closed her eyes, and for a mad moment she could imagine him brushing her lips with a rosebud, until her mouth parted and he dipped his head to kiss her...

Oh, for pity's sake. This mooning around had to stop. She needed to be *sensible*.

OK, so she'd managed to talk her mother and her grandmother round on the subject of her arranged marriage, but that didn't mean that she could have a future with Liam.

Then again, he'd sent her the photograph.

Was he expecting a reply? Hoping for a reply? Waiting to see what she did next?

Why hadn't he sent her a proper message? Traditionally, a red rose meant true love, so was this his declaration?

And what should she say to him?

She shook herself. Ridiculous. She'd been training for her role for so long. She knew exactly what to do and say in almost every situation, and she was bright enough to work out what to do in situations that were new to her.

Except this one. Because she couldn't think straight where Liam MacCarthy was concerned.

He'd sent her a picture without a comment. So perhaps she should do the same.

She'd picked up a shell from the beach on

that last day. She fished it out of the drawer where she'd stored it, took a snap of it on her phone, and sent it to him without a single word of explanation.

A seashell?

What on earth did Vittoria mean by a seashell? Liam wondered.

He remembered that she'd picked one up from the beach on their last afternoon together. After he'd told her that he wasn't looking for a relationship. Had she sent him a picture of the shell to remind him of that conversation? Or was it a reminder of their first evening on the beach near the dunes, when they'd watched the stars come out and he'd kissed her? Or maybe it was a warning, a reminder of that last morning, when they'd woken together in the room with the view of the sea and agreed that this was goodbye.

He drummed his fingers on his desk as he thought about it. The longer he dwelt on it, the less he could work out what it meant.

It was his own fault. He'd been the one to start this, sending her a picture without a caption. A picture was meant to be worth a thousand words. This seashell was the equivalent of two single-spaced A4 pages of text. Was he reading things into the picture that weren't there? What was she trying to say to him?

And what did he want to reply?

The obvious thing to do would be to send a photograph of a bluebell. But flowers, he knew, had meanings. Everyone knew what a red rose meant, but what about bluebells? He needed to be sure that he wasn't sending her the wrong message. Checking online told him that the bluebell was a legally protected flower in England—who knew what she'd make of that?—and that in the language of flowers it was a symbol of constancy and everlasting love.

Two flowers in a row, expressing love. Wooing her with flower photographs. Wooing her, when he knew it couldn't possibly work out between them. The princess and the photographer. They were worlds and worlds apart. This was insanity.

But he couldn't get Vittoria out of his head. He thought about her all the time. And he had a nasty feeling that this weird feeling, the one he couldn't pin down, might just be the 'everlasting love' signified by a bluebell.

And he really didn't know what to do about *that*.

Knowing it wasn't a sensible idea, he sent the photograph to her.

* * *

Bluebells?

Vittoria stared at the picture.

It was an English bluebell, with narrow bells down one side of the stem only. Liam was definitely reminding her of their conversation that last morning. When he'd told her he wished he'd asked her to take out the brown contact lenses in the woods, because her eyes were the same colour as the bluebells.

Were they the same colour as bluebells?

She left her desk and headed for the bathroom, where she stared at herself in the mirror.

Eyes the colour of bluebells…

She and Liam hadn't spoken since he'd dropped her at Izzy's flat. They'd agreed that it was over. Neither of them had messaged the other—except for his email to her with the access code for his website, the brief exchange when he'd thanked her for the book, and now the photographs.

What was he telling her, this time?

And what should she reply?

She went back to her desk and logged in to the private gallery on his website. Then she zoomed in on one of the photographs she'd taken of him in the bluebell wood.

He'd said that a portrait showed you who someone was.

He'd also said that these were pretty much stock male portrait poses.

And here he was, his right hand up so it almost cupped his chin, his thumb to the side and his index finger across his slightly pouted lips.

Almost as if he were saying, 'Shh.' Telling her what she was seeing was secret.

There was a glint in his eye. Like a mischievous little boy?

Or was that glint something else? His feelings, something he didn't want to tell and wanted to keep secret?

She zoomed in on his eyes. Beautiful eyes: with long, long lashes and tiny crinkles at the corner. Were they telling her his feelings for her?

He had a beautiful mouth, too. And when she remembered how that mouth had made her feel, she went hot all over.

She wanted to wake up in his arms again. Wanted him there with her, teasing her and laughing with her and making love with her.

But even if he felt the same—even if he was prepared to change his career plans to fit in with her life—would it be fair to ask him to do that? To be with her, Liam would need to move from London to San Rocello. Away from his sister, away from his work, away from the home he'd built over the years.

She'd be asking him to give up so much.

Just like his old girlfriends who'd resented him spending his time with Saoirse or building his career. Although Vittoria didn't want to be the be-all and end-all of his life—for her, too, family was important, and she wanted him to be able to follow his ambitions—her role as queen would have to come first. There wasn't a middle way, however she looked at it.

Even if she did let him come to her, even if he was willing to give up everything she asked him to—was she making the same mistake again? Would he, like Rufus, realise the royal life wasn't for him and back away?

Maybe it was better to say nothing. To bury her hopes intact, instead of having them crushed. To leave it as a might-have-been. Instead of acting on the temptation to reply, to find a picture of a cornflower and send it to him to continue the flirting by flowers, she went back to reading the report she'd been working on before his message arrived.

No reply.

Maybe she was busy, Liam told himself.

But three more days without a reply told

him that either Vittoria didn't want to play this game any more, or she didn't like whatever she'd read into his last message.

It was what they'd agreed anyway that night. A one-off. Not to be repeated.

He'd been stupid to wish it could be otherwise.

CHAPTER SEVEN

VITTORIA WOKE, FEELING NAUSEOUS.

She must've eaten something at the reception last night that had disagreed with her.

But sipping cold water didn't help with the nausea, which seemed to come in waves. The idea of coffee—which she loved—made her feel worse. Even the smell of it was disgusting, and she left her mug untouched.

She felt dreadful all morning. Maybe she was going down with some kind of bug. Or maybe she was going to get poetic justice for the fib she'd told to the private secretary about having the period from hell, to get those few sneaky days away, and she really *was* going to have the period from h—

She went cold.

Period.

Hers were regular practically to the hour.

And it should have started yesterday morning.

She dragged in a breath. She was being

ridiculous. There were dozens of reasons why her period might be late, or why she might miss one altogether. Besides, that one night she'd spent with Liam, they'd been sensible. They'd used condoms.

A little voice in her head reminded her that the only one hundred per cent guaranteed form of contraception was abstinence.

The risk of a condom failing to protect her was tiny. So tiny as to be almost negligible.

But even a tiny risk was still an actual risk.

And a missed period plus feeling sick added up to something that scared her so much, her skin felt too tight.

Vittoria was out of sorts all day. She wanted to go out and buy a pregnancy test so she could prove to herself that she was being ridiculous and of course she wasn't pregnant. But there was no way she could purchase a pregnancy test herself. Someone would notice what she was buying, someone might tell the press—and, with modern technology making the rumour mill work globally twenty-four-seven, all sorts of stories would be flying round the world within seconds. Speculation as to whether Princess Vittoria was pregnant, who the father might be, and why she'd kept the relationship secret from her family and her friends…

But she also didn't want to put that kind of burden on any of her staff. Swearing them to secrecy and asking them to go and buy a pregnancy test for her really wouldn't be fair.

If she went to the palace doctor, her mother or her grandparents would know about it; they'd worry and start asking questions. And no way could she confide in her mother or her grandmother. Apart from the fact that she knew how disappointed they'd be, they'd only just agreed to stop smothering her in cotton wool. This news would definitely wreck the new relationship she was trying to forge with them. If she couldn't be trusted not to get accidentally pregnant, how could she be trusted to choose her own consort?

Vittoria had never felt more isolated in her life. With only a small family, and her close friends not even living in the same country—she couldn't remember when they'd last managed to get together—there was nobody she could turn to.

Buying a test online and having it delivered wasn't an option, because all the palace post was screened.

The more she thought about it, the more panicky she felt.

She still hadn't found a solution by the evening. And when her mobile phone rang with a video call and she saw Izzy's name flash up on screen, she nearly didn't answer—she didn't want her sister to see her in such a state. But just ignoring the call and pretending to be busy wasn't fair to Izzy. Her sister's last exam had been that morning and she wanted to congratulate her.

Forcing herself to sound bright, Vittoria answered the call. 'Hey, it's my favourite sister. How are you?'

'Brilliant. Free from exams for ever!'

'Congratulations, that's great. I assume you're going out tonight to celebrate the end of Finals?'

'Sursh and I are going out for champagne,' Izzy said.

And how pathetic was it that Vittoria found herself wondering where Liam was, or if he'd be buying the girls celebratory champagne?

'Rina? Are you OK?'

'Yes, of course,' she lied. For pity's sake. Where was her impassive royal face when she needed it?

'You don't look it,' Izzy said. 'You looked worried sick. Is it Nonno?'

'No, he's fine,' Vittoria hastened to reassure her.

'Then what's wrong?'

To her horror, Vittoria felt a tear slide down her cheek. And, of course, Izzy noticed it.

'You're crying. Is it Mamma? Have she and Nonna changed their minds and they're trying to make you marry José?'

'No.' Vittoria closed her eyes. 'Iz, I might...' The words stuck in her throat.

'Right. I'm getting the next flight over,' Izzy said. 'Or the overnight train, if there isn't a flight.'

'No! It's...' Vittoria forced herself to breathe. 'I just... I might be pregnant.'

'*Pregnant?* How?'

'Shh. You know how this stuff works.'

'I mean who?'

'Are you alone?' Vittoria asked, panic coursing through her as a nasty thought hit her. If Saoirse was there and overheard any of this, and she told her brother...

'Sursh has just gone home to change.'

Thank God. 'You can't tell *anyone* about this. Anyone at all. Promise me.'

'I promise.' Izzy frowned. 'Have you done a test?'

'Not yet.' And she desperately wanted to. She needed to know for sure. 'But I can't go and buy one myself. I can't see the doctor without Mamma finding out and worrying. You know the post is checked so I can't buy one online, and I can't put that kind of burden on any of the staff.'

'That's easily sorted. I'll get one,' Izzy said, 'and I'll bring it to you.'

'That's ridiculous. I can't ask you to do that.'

'You're in a muddle and you need someone to lean on,' Izzy said. 'Which would be me. You've always been there for me. Let me be there for you, Rina.'

'But you've got Finals celebrations with your friends.'

'What's more important? A party, or the person I love most in the whole world?'

And now Vittoria really was crying. Even though her sister was hundreds of miles away, right at that moment she didn't feel alone. 'You can't get here tonight. There isn't a commercial flight and I can't send a private plane over.' Not without a lot of explanations she wasn't ready to give. 'Go to your party.'

'Then I'll get it tomorrow and bring it,' Izzy said, undaunted.

'Love you, Iz.'

'Love you, too. Now, stop panicking. You might not even be pregnant. It might be stress making you late,' Izzy said. 'How late are you?'

'A day. Which I know sounds utterly ridiculous, but I'm regular to the hour, Iz. I always have been.'

Izzy was clearly counting backwards in her head, because she said, 'So if you are pregnant, it happened while you were in Engl— Oh, my God. Are you telling me it's Liam's?'

Adrenalin coursed through her veins. 'Iz, you promised not to say anything to anyone.'

'And I won't. But, if you *are* pregnant, you need to talk to him,' Izzy warned.

'I know,' Vittoria said miserably. It wasn't a conversation she wanted to have.

'You did use protection, didn't you?'

'Of course we did.' She dragged in a breath. 'But obviously something went wrong.'

'Oh, Rina. Look, it's going to be OK,' Izzy said, 'and I'll get the first flight home tomorrow. We'll sort it out.'

Vittoria thought wryly that her little sister sounded very much like her. Except this time, it would be her scatty little sister rescuing her, not the other way round.

'Try to get some rest,' Izzy said, for all the world as if she were the elder sister. 'I'm not going to say a word to anyone. And I love you. Whatever the result is, whatever you decide, I've got your back.'

That love and protectiveness only made Vittoria want to cry even more.

'Don't worry. It's going to be fine,' Izzy said. 'I love you.'

Somehow Vittoria got through the rest of the evening, along with a morning where she couldn't face her morning coffee and panicked even more. And then Izzy was there, breezing into the palace and smothering everyone in hugs. 'Just a fleeting visit—a bit of post-exams homesickness,' she explained to their mother and grandparents. And, as soon as she could, she swept Vittoria up to her room. 'I need a proper catch-up with my big sister,' she announced.

As soon as the door to Vittoria's suite was closed, Izzy hugged her. 'All righty. Time to pee on a stick.'

'How did you get the test?' Vittoria asked. If Izzy had asked Saoirse to buy it, and Saoirse had made the connection…

'I asked Pietro to get it,' Izzy said. 'And he won't be telling. He doesn't know who it's for, just that it's not for me.'

'Thank you.' It felt as if half a ton of rocks had fallen from her shoulders.

Izzy handed over the little box. 'So how long has this thing between you and Liam gone on? Since your official photograph?'

Vittoria shook her head. 'There was a point in the photo shoot where I thought he was going to kiss me—when he took those pictures for you. And then he took another shot. A more private one.'

'Can I see?'

Considering how much her sister had already done for her, it would be churlish to say no. Vittoria logged into the private portfolio, then handed over her phone. 'Look for yourself. I need to do that test.'

Pregnant or not pregnant?

She peed on the stick and waited, her breath shallow; her heart felt as if it was beating so loudly that the whole palace could hear.

Time seemed to drag. For pity's sake, how long was two minutes?

But finally there was a blue line to tell her that the test was working. She stared at the other window, willing it to stay blank.

If it was blank, meaning she wasn't pregnant, then she had time to think about what she wanted to do. Time to think about how she felt.

If there was a second line…then everything would change. What then? Was San Rocello progressive enough to accept the idea that their new queen would be a single mum? She rather thought not.

What other options were there?

Termination was the obvious one. She'd never judge another woman for taking that option—everyone's circumstances were different, and you had to make your own decision based on your personal circumstances. But it wasn't the option she wanted for herself.

Liam had a right to know about the baby; but he'd already told her that he didn't want to bring up a family because he'd done that already with Saoirse. So she was pretty sure that, although he was attracted to her and he'd do his best to support her, he wouldn't actually want to make a family with her.

Which brought her back to being a single mum.

If she wasn't the queen-in-waiting, nobody would bat an eyelid about her pregnancy or the baby.

But, in her situation, it would be a political minefield.

How on earth would she tell her family? They'd be devastated.

She realised then that she was staring unseeing at the stick, not focusing on the little window. She blinked and narrowed her eyes at it.

There was a second blue line. A strong one.

Underlining that she'd taken a risk, been reckless, and lost.

And then she was promptly sick, retching until her stomach was empty and her face was clammy.

Once she'd washed her face and hands and disposed of the test stick, she headed back out to Izzy.

Her sister took one look at her and wrapped her arms round her. 'Oh, Rina.'

'Positive,' Vittoria whispered.

'It's very early days. Four or five weeks since the start of your last period,' Izzy said thoughtfully. 'OK. The important thing here is what *you* want to do.'

'Mamma and Nonna—they'll be so disappointed in me. So angry.'

'We'll deal with that later. Right now, we need to focus on you.' Izzy blew out a breath. 'Are you going to tell Liam?'

Vittoria nodded. 'He has a right to know. And, I guess, to be part of the decision.'

'But he doesn't have the right to pressure you into anything you don't want to do,' Izzy warned.

'You know him.' Ironically, probably better than Vittoria did. 'He's not like that.'

'So tell me exactly how things are between you,' Izzy said. 'I looked at all the pictures in that file. The ones he took of you, where you're all starry-eyed and blossoming, and the ones you took of him, where he looks as if he can't take his eyes off you.'

'We didn't set out to have a fling. He was

just being kind, giving me a bit of space—I don't know, maybe paying it forward because someone gave him a break when he was struggling. Except I was so aware of him, Iz. And when he kissed me under the stars, that first night at the cottage, it felt like a hundred rainbows blooming in my head, and I forgot everything else in the world. We didn't go to bed together that night—but we grew closer. And that last night, we…' She spread her hands. 'It just felt right. And waking up with him, the next day.' Even thinking about it made her miss him.

'Does he know how you feel about him?'

'You know him, Iz. You know he's observant, because of what he does for a living. And you just said I look starry-eyed in those photographs. He must've seen it, too.'

'OK. I'll ask the hard question. Do you know how he feels about you?'

'No.' How could she be so clueless? She was meant to be taking over the running of a country, and right now she was making a total mess of her own life.

Izzy hugged her. 'I can see in your face that you're beating yourself up. Don't. If it helps, since I've known Liam, there hasn't been anyone special in his life. He dates, but not very seriously. He's really focused on his work—

even more than you are.' She paused. 'I don't think he takes people to his cottage, either, except for his best friend. So that has to count for something.'

When had her little sister grown up and become so wise? Or was Vittoria as guilty as her mother and grandmother of treating Izzy as if she was much younger than she really was?

'We agreed it can't work. He's got his career and I'm going to be queen. And he's not from our world, Iz. It's a lot to cope with if you haven't been brought up in it.'

'If the guy really loves you, he'll make it work. He'll learn whatever skills he needs so he can deal with life at the palace,' Izzy said. 'Just because Rufus couldn't do it, it doesn't mean that Liam can't.'

'He was very clear about the fact he doesn't want a relationship. He's already done the parenting thing with Saoirse—though he was clear about the fact he didn't regret that, either,' Vittoria added swiftly. 'But he wants to focus on his career.'

'Do you think your news might change his mind?' Izzy asked.

'I don't know. But I don't want him to feel he's under any obligation,' Vittoria said.

'So what you're saying is that you want

him to be with you and the baby, but only because he wants to be there?' Izzy asked gently.

'I want someone who sees me for who I am and loves me for that. Not someone who has to learn to love me because I'm going to be the queen and he's going to be my consort.'

'Anything else is second-best—and you're worth more than that,' Izzy said. 'Have you talked since you've been back at the palace?'

Vittoria wrinkled her nose. 'Not exactly.'

'Why not?'

'There wasn't any point. It was a fling. It's over.'

'But?' Izzy asked gently.

'He did send me an email with the password to the private gallery, and two photographs. A red rose, first, and then a bluebell.'

'A red rose and a bluebell? What's that supposed to mean?' Izzy asked.

'I don't know. I sent him a picture of a seashell.'

Izzy shook her head. 'Oh, my God. You're as bad as each other. Just talk to each other and stop playing games. It sounds to me as if you've both made all these big speeches about not having a future together, and you've both painted yourself into a corner, and neither of you knows what to say now. I bet you're both waiting for the other to make the next move. Stop letting pride or whatever get in the way. Go and see him. Talk. Be honest.'

'What if he doesn't feel the same way?'

'Then we'll deal with it. I've got your back. If he doesn't love you, though, he's an idiot and he doesn't deserve you.'

The indignant look on her sister's face made Vittoria smile. 'I love you, Iz. Thank you.'

But, all the same, she worried.

How was Liam going to react? She didn't have a clue. She didn't really know him that well. Those moments of connection between them in England had taken her breath away; but would they be enough to sustain a relationship, especially one that would be lived out in the very public world of the San Rocello royal family?

There was only one way to find out.

She definitely wasn't going to tell him the news by text, by phone or even by video call. This was something that needed to be said face to face. She needed to see his reaction, to know how he really felt.

It took Vittoria a while to find the right words—until after Izzy had gone back to London—but she kept her text simple.

Need to talk to you about something face to face. Where/when are you available in the next week?

And now the ball was in his court.

Need to talk to you about something face to face. Where/when are you available in the next week?

Liam looked at the text and frowned.

What did Vittoria need to talk to him about? And why did it have to be face to face? Had someone found out about their fling and it was going to cause a scandal? But neither of them was dating anyone else, and he knew she'd decided to stand up to her family about the arranged marriage issue. So, even if their fling had been leaked, he couldn't see what the problem was.

He texted back.

Is everything all right?

Of course. Is there a window in your diary?

She sounded cool, calm, collected and extremely businesslike.

Not the woman behind the tiara who'd

melted into his arms. Not the woman whose smile was like sunshine. Not the woman whose eyes reminded him of spring bluebells.

A window in his diary, indeed. Anyone would think this was a business meeting. Though, if it was—if she wanted him to take some other portraits—surely she would've given him an idea about the brief?

Which meant this had to be personal. And it stung that she was being so formal with him. They'd spent the night together, woken in each other's arms. Had it really meant so little to her? OK, they'd agreed to regard it as a fling and they'd said goodbye. But he'd wondered if there was a way of finding a compromise. Surely it hadn't been completely one-sided?

He thought about it some more.

He hadn't heard anything through Saoirse or Izzy, both of whom were planning to go up to Edinburgh tomorrow to see an art exhibition. He hadn't seen any rumours in the news.

So what exactly did the future Queen of San Rocello want with him?

There was only one way to find out. He checked his diary.

Have location shoots in London Mon/Wed/Fri. Planned dark room sessions Tuesday and Thursday. Can work round those.

Tuesday works for me. I'll book a meeting room at a hotel and let you know the venue.

This definitely sounded like business; he'd been deluding himself that it might be personal. There hadn't been a hint of warmth in her texts. No kiss used as punctuation at the end of a message. No more flirting by photograph—she still hadn't replied to his bluebell. The soft, sweet, slightly shy woman he'd spent time with on the coast had turned back into an efficient machine. The Winter Queen.

And that hurt.

Well, he could be a machine, too.

Meeting room good for me. Let me know location and time.

He didn't add a kiss to soften the message or make it less impersonal.

But he was out of sorts for the rest of the day. Brooding. Wondering what she wanted from him—and whether he was prepared to deal with the formal princess, rather than the woman he'd escaped to the seaside with.

And on Tuesday he'd find out what she wanted.

CHAPTER EIGHT

A BUSINESS MEETING.

What did you wear to a business meeting with a princess? Liam wondered.

He'd worn a suit to the palace when he'd gone to shoot Vittoria's official portrait; he'd worn faded jeans when he'd taken her to the beach and kissed her. Neither extreme felt right for this. And Vittoria still hadn't given him a clue what this was about, even though he'd asked her explicitly if there was a brief or anything in particular he needed to bring to the meeting. Subtle questioning of Izzy hadn't given him any more information.

So maybe he'd simply go as his professional self. The confident and competent portrait photographer whose outfit on a shoot made him practically invisible. Black designer jeans, a silky black long-sleeved top, black shoes. And he took his laptop and compact camera with him, just in case.

The hotel she'd chosen was near a Tube station. He left himself extra time to get there, in case of delays, but everything ran on schedule. There was a big difference between arriving a couple of minutes early for a meeting in order not to waste any time, and turning up so early that you appeared desperate and hampered yourself in any negotiations. So he found the nearest coffee shop, bought a double espresso, set an alarm on his phone to make sure he didn't lose track of time and end up being late, and settled down in a corner to work on some post-production stuff on his laptop.

When his phone vibrated to warn him it was time to leave, he made his way to the hotel where the receptionist gave him directions to the meeting room. He rapped on the door and walked in. It was an anonymous room with cream-coloured walls, a corporate blue carpet, a rectangular oak table with eight executive office chairs, and a large screen which was obviously for use with a laptop and presentation software.

Vittoria was sitting at the head of the table with a glass of water in front of her, Giorgio to one side. His heart actually skipped a beat at seeing her again.

'Thank you for coming, Mr MacCarthy.' Her voice and her expression were both inscrutable.

She could honestly be this formal, this cool with him, after the night they'd shared together? After waking up with him, with her expression all soft and sensual?

The pleasure he'd felt at seeing her drained away, and his skin suddenly felt too tight. OK, so maybe it had been unrealistic to expect her to fall into his arms—they'd agreed that night was a one-off. But he had expected some warmth from her. He didn't understand why she was freezing him out. Why was he even here?

'You're welcome, *Vostra Altezza Reale.*' He used the formal phrase deliberately, pushing back at the woman who was clearly in full regal mode. *Your Royal Highness.*

'May I order you some coffee? Something cold?'

The coldest thing in the room, he thought, was Vittoria herself. Polite and utterly inscrutable. And he still didn't know why she'd asked him to meet her. 'I'm fine, thank you, ma'am.'

She gave a small signal to Giorgio, who left the room.

This was starting to feel a little surreal. Why would she ask her security detail to give them privacy? She trusted Giorgio literally with her life; surely it wouldn't matter if he heard any confidential business matters?

'What did you want to discuss?' he asked. And why had she been so insistent on this meeting being face to face?

'How are you?' she asked, not answering his question.

Frustrated. Churned up. Feeling as if something was about to drop on his head from a great height. So, instead of giving her an anodyne answer and asking an equally polite but meaningless question, he took the direct route. 'Right now I'm very much in the dark about why you wanted to see me. Isn't this something that we could've talked about over the phone or a video call?'

'No.'

Then he noticed how pale she looked, and frowned. She'd asked him how he was, but he hadn't asked her how she was. And, although her make-up was flawless and someone who barely knew her would just think she was being regal, on closer inspection he thought she looked tense. Upset. And it took the fight out of him, because now all he wanted to do was hold her close. Protect her. Tell her that whatever was wrong, he'd be by her side and he'd help her get through whatever it was. 'Are you all right, Vittoria?' he asked gently, completely forgetting protocol.

'I…' She dragged in a breath. 'Sit down, Liam. Please.'

Now he was worried.

Was she ill? Seriously ill? *Terminally* ill?

Was she going to ask him and Saoirse to help her prepare Izzy for some terrible news?

He sat down and forced himself to breathe. And he waited for her to fill the silence—to tell him what she wanted.

Seeing Liam again made Vittoria's heart do a backflip. He was dressed as a professional photographer, all in black so it would make him practically invisible at a shoot and he could blend into any background.

Except he was far from being invisible to her. She was acutely aware of him.

Those beautiful eyes.

That gorgeous mouth.

The hands that had held her close, cherished her.

And now she was going to have to tell him her news. She still had no idea how he'd react, though in her head she'd gone over every possible reaction he might have and worked out how to respond. Shock. Anger. Dismay.

The only reaction she hadn't bothered to think about was delight, because she already knew he wasn't going to be delighted about this. If you'd made it perfectly clear that you didn't want to settle down and have a family, then obviously you weren't going to be too thrilled at the idea of becoming a parent.

'I wanted to tell you in person,' she said, 'because I think you have the right to know.' She took a deep breath. 'I'm pregnant.'

What?

Liam stared at her in shock, trying to process what she'd just told him.

It was the last thing he'd expected to hear.

Pregnant?

She couldn't possibly be.

'You're pregnant,' he said, just to check that he'd heard her correctly.

She said nothing, simply inclined her head. And he couldn't see Vittoria behind her mask. All he could see was the princess, coolly telling him that they'd accidentally made a baby when they'd spent that night together.

He certainly didn't think it was anyone else's baby. But he still couldn't quite get his head round this. 'We were careful. We used condoms.'

'There's always a tiny, tiny chance that contraception won't work.' She spread her hands. 'Unfortunately, we were that chance.'

He shook his head, trying to clear it. He'd resisted every girlfriend who wanted him to settle down and raise a family; the way he saw it, he'd already done that with Saoirse. Now was the time when he'd wanted to focus on his career. He was clear about his goals and he knew how to get there. He was putting the work in.

But Vittoria was pregnant.

With his baby.

And *that* changed everything.

He could be selfish. Walk away. Stick to his original plans and focus on his career.

But if he did that, he'd lose his self-respect.

Which meant there was only one choice.

He was about to open his mouth and ask her if she was sure, if she'd done a pregnancy test—but of course Vittoria di Sarda would've done a test. She wouldn't be sitting here if the test hadn't been positive.

Now he thought he understood why she'd asked Giorgio for privacy. Not to protect her, but to protect *him* when she delivered news that she knew would shock him to the core.

She was pregnant.

With his baby.

The words repeated over and over in his head.

What did he do now? What did he say? Did she want to keep the baby? Did she want him to bring the baby up with her?

I wanted to tell you in person because I think you have the right to know.

That didn't give him a clue about her feelings or what she wanted. Was she telling him that this was a royal baby so, although he had the right to know of the baby's existence, she didn't plan to acknowledge him as the father? Or was she being proud, expecting him to reject her and being cool with him so she could protect her heart?

He had no idea.

And what did he want?

He'd worked hard to build his career, from the very lowest rung. He wouldn't be able to fit that round supporting Vittoria in her royal duties; he'd have to give it up. Move away from London, away from his sister. And that was assuming her family would even accept him as her partner, which he doubted very much. Vittoria's mother and grandmother wanted her to marry the son of a Spanish duke, so it was pretty obvious how they'd react to the idea of her settling down with someone without a single drop of blue blood in his veins.

He didn't have a clue what to say.

All he knew was that Vittoria was pregnant with his baby.

And that he'd never, ever shirk his responsibilities.

'Obviously I'll do the right thing,' he said. 'I'll stand by you.'

* * *

Breathe. Don't cry. Don't let the hormones take over, Vittoria warned herself.

She knew that Liam didn't want to settle down and bring up a family. He'd told her why, that night when they'd talked under the stars. The night they'd really connected. *The night they'd made the baby.* Over the last few days, since she'd tried to work out how he'd react, she'd expected him to walk away.

Though it wasn't until he'd spoken that Vittoria realised what she'd wanted him to say. Deep down, she'd wanted him to tell her that he'd changed his mind about having a family— that he loved her, that he wanted to bring up their baby with her. Make a family with her.

What he'd actually said was that he'd do the right thing. That he'd stand by her.

That, if anything, was worse than the arranged marriage her mother and grandmother had been planning before she'd met Liam. Because it meant his decision to stay with her was all about duty and nothing to do with love.

He'd been here before, parenting his younger sister; and he'd been very clear that he'd walked away from university and his own chances because he'd loved his sister. He found Vittoria physically attractive—the baby, she thought wryly, was proof of that—but he didn't love her.

And that was the deciding factor.

She wouldn't settle for anything less than love. So she'd give him what he'd said he wanted. Freedom to pursue his career.

'There's no need to "stand by me", as you put it. It's the twenty-first century,' she said crisply. 'I'm perfectly capable of raising this baby alone. I have the resources.' Not that money could ever take the place of love, but she wouldn't be struggling financially and could afford to pay for the kind of nanny who'd bring joy into a child's life while Vittoria was working. Izzy would stand by her. And eventually her mother and her grandparents would come around.

And she'd do it all without Liam beside her.

Hurt that Liam clearly saw her and the baby only as a duty, she hit back in the only way she knew how. With coolness. 'You don't need to be involved in the slightest.'

'You don't need to be involved in the slightest.'

The words felt like a physical blow.

Was Vittoria saying she didn't want Liam to be involved? That she didn't think he was good enough to be the father of a prince or princess?

Together, they'd created a life. They had responsibilities—to each other and to their child. Did she really think he'd walk away from that? Did she really believe he was that selfish?

Well, she could think again. No way was his child going to be brought up by a string of nannies in a distant corner of the palace where they wouldn't be seen or heard by the royal family, the way he was pretty sure Vittoria had been brought up. His child would be loved—the way he and Saoirse had been loved, during the few years they'd had their parents.

He folded his arms. 'I'm sure we can come to some kind of custody arrangement.'

She looked shocked, then. 'You want custody of the baby?'

'This baby's mine as well as yours,' he pointed out. 'I didn't dump my sister in a boarding school because it would've been more convenient for me to do so, and I'm certainly not planning to do that with my child. So I suggest our child spends weekdays with me in London, and weekends and some school holidays with you. I'm sure any lawyer would agree with me, because clearly you'll have royal duties to fulfil—which means you won't be around for much of the time.'

'You want custody,' she repeated, as if she couldn't quite believe what he'd said.

'I want to be there when my child grows up. I remember having two parents, but I also remember what it was like growing up with a single parent. And I have experience of rearing children, because I've acted as a parent to my little sister.'

'I know you gave up university for Saoirse.' Vittoria dragged in a breath. 'But you said you didn't want to get involved with anyone, that you didn't want to settle down and start a family, because you wanted to focus on your career.'

'Which is correct. But I'm at a place in my career,' he said, 'where I don't have to chase after people. I can set the parameters. So I'll accept appointments for shoots only when my child is at school.'

'What if a shoot overruns?'

That was an easy one. 'They won't. The contracts will have the kind of penalty clauses that'll make even the most difficult of clients stick rigidly to the schedule.'

'What if the shoot's abroad?'

He shrugged. 'Either I'll turn the job down, or I'll reschedule it for a time when my child is staying with you.'

'You'd give up your career for the baby.'

'I'd work around my baby,' he corrected. 'Which makes it the best of both worlds. It means my baby has a dad and will know he or she is dearly loved; and meanwhile my career carries on as I planned.'

She frowned. 'But you said you didn't want responsibilities.'

'That was then. The situation's different now. Like it or not, we made a baby. And that's a game-changer.'

Where had this hard, cold stranger come from? There wasn't a hint of a smile in those corn-flower-blue eyes. Where was the man who'd told her that her smile was like sunshine, the man who'd carried her up two flights of stairs to her bed?

And why did he keep calling the baby *his* child? The baby was *theirs*. And she was the one who was carrying the baby, not him.

'Do you have a problem with that?' he enquired.

Yes. She had a lot of problems with it.

And he hadn't even asked her how she was feeling—if she'd got morning sickness, if she was bone-deep tired all the time, if her feet were puffy or if maybe she wanted a hug because she was tearful and struggling to deal with the hormones.

Nothing.

Obviously she'd just been a fling to him. Casual. Meaningless.

And all that business of quoting poetry at her, at making her laugh in the bluebells and holding her close on the beach, kissing her under the stars—it had been mere flirtation to him. Just sex. Nothing deeper.

What a fool she'd been.

Particularly as he'd even told her straight out that he didn't do relationships. He'd been honest with her. She'd been very stupid to think her news might change his mind.

Well, it *had* changed his mind.

Just not in the way she'd expected. It seemed that now he wanted the baby—but he didn't want her.

And that hurt.

That *really* hurt.

She'd thought he understood her. That they'd had a connection. But she'd been oh, so wrong.

He hadn't suggested trying to bring the baby up together. Because he didn't love her? Or because it was the same situation as Rufus all over again—that he didn't want to be constrained by the restrictions of a royal lifestyle?

She'd never thought of herself as a coward, but she couldn't bring herself to ask him if they could work this out together. She didn't want him to see her as his duty. She wanted to be loved. And she couldn't see a single sign of love in the man facing her across the table.

A queen never shows her feelings, she reminded herself. Cool, calm, collected. That was the order of the day.

'I'll give the palace lawyer your details. Perhaps you can put her in touch with your lawyer and they can come up with a workable solution between them,' she said, standing up and pushing her chair back. 'I don't think there's anything left to say. Goodbye, Mr MacCarthy.' She just about resisted a sarcastic, 'Have a nice day.'

And she walked out of the meeting room with her chin held high, every inch the princess. Because she wasn't going to give Liam MacCarthy the satisfaction of crying her eyes out and begging him to love her and their baby, so he could reject her all over again.

Liam stayed where he was as the door closed behind her, feeling as if he'd just been squashed by a steamroller.

What the hell had just happened?

Two weeks ago, he'd spent a few days in a secluded cottage near the beach with a woman who'd made his heart beat faster: a woman who was out of his reach, but he'd wanted her anyway. The more he'd got to know her, the more he'd liked her and the more he'd found himself falling in love with her. To the point where he'd broken some of his own rules and carried her to bed on that last night.

They were from different worlds. He knew that. She had responsibilities she couldn't walk away from—well, technically she could walk away, but he knew she loved Izzy and wouldn't dump those responsibilities on her sister. And he didn't come from a world where you needed a bodyguard, or where the world was watching you all the time, waiting for you to put a single foot wrong. But he'd hoped that maybe they'd find a way to bridge that gap—that they'd find a way together. He'd started flirting with her by photographs, and he'd been delighted when she'd flirted back. It had given him hope that they might just have a chance of working things out between them.

But then she'd closed off. He'd assumed her silence meant she'd thought about it and changed her mind.

And now she'd summoned him for a royal audience. There was no other way to describe what this meeting had just been.

According to her, he had the right to the knowledge that she was expecting his baby, but he didn't need to be involved with the child in the slightest. She'd suggested that his lawyer should get in touch with hers to come up with a workable solution.

It made him so angry that he wanted to punch something.

This was a *baby* they were talking about, not a piece of property.

If she was going to take that kind of attitude, why hadn't she just communicated through her lawyer in the first place? Or delegated the task to the palace secretary? Why had she asked him to meet her face to face?

He had no idea. But she'd made it clear she didn't want him. That night under the stars, she'd told him she wanted a partner who loved her—a partner she loved back.

Obviously, she hadn't meant him. That flare of desire between them had been just that: desire. Sexual attraction. Nothing that involved deeper emotions. He'd been stupid to hope otherwise.

If she'd wanted him, she would've said so. Or at least shown some warmth. But she'd been every inch the unapproachable queen-to-be. She wanted to communicate with him only through their lawyers.

And he was shocked to realise how much that hurt.

Vittoria was expecting his baby. They could have made a family—something he knew they both missed. And for a second he could almost see their child at the beach, building a sandcastle: a little girl with her mother's smile and amazing eyes, and his own unruly hair. Vittoria herself, barefoot and smiling at the scene, her knees drawn up and her hands clasped loosely by her ankles. A dog next to her, with his chin resting on her feet. Himself, capturing the joy of the moment with his camera, and then going over to his wife and kissing her...

He blinked the vision away. Stupid. It wasn't going to happen like that. And how utterly ironic that he'd only realised what he really wanted when it was completely out of his reach.

'Where to now, ma'am?' Giorgio asked.

'The airport,' Vittoria said.

'I'll have the car brought round,' he said. 'Do you need anything while we wait?'

Yes. She needed Liam. But he'd made it clear he didn't want her. 'I'm fine, thank you.'

She didn't say a word on the drive back to the airport. She just about remembered to thank the driver—being a royal meant having good manners, not being rude and entitled and taking things for granted.

To her relief, the private flight meant using a different entrance to the airport and an extremely quick boarding time. Although their flight time couldn't be moved, being on the plane was much better than being stuck waiting in the airport. One step closer to home.

'Rina.' Giorgio almost never used her pet name, but right at that moment he took her hand and was looking concerned, almost like a big brother. 'I might be speaking out of turn, but is there anything I can do?'

'Thanks, but I'm fine,' she fibbed.

'No, you're not,' he said softly. 'I've known you for more than a decade.'

She knew what he was being too tactful to say. The last time she'd been this upset was when Rufus had walked out on her. For a moment, she considered confiding in her security detail—but it wouldn't be fair to burden him.

'OK. I'm not fine,' she admitted, 'but I will be.' She'd have to be fine. There was no other choice.

Their country might not approve of her being a single mum, but they'd all have to make the best of it. And she'd have to learn to stop yearning for something she couldn't have. Stop wishing for love. Maybe her mother and grandmother were right after all; for a royal, an arranged marriage was the only workable option. This whole thing with Liam had underlined that a relationship with someone not from a royal background would only end in tears.

CHAPTER NINE

WITH HIS SISTER in Edinburgh, it meant Liam didn't have to put on an act and pretend nothing was wrong. He could just go straight into his darkroom and bury himself in work—because at least if he did something where he had to concentrate, he wouldn't have the headspace to think about Vittoria. Vittoria and their baby.

At least, that was the theory. In practice, he couldn't concentrate, and even developing some simple prints appeared to be beyond him. Everything he touched went wrong and he had to repeat everything.

Eventually, there was a tight band of tension across his eyes, and he had to acknowledge defeat. But when he went downstairs to make himself some coffee, he could hear chattering—and he could smell pizza.

He walked into the kitchen. 'I thought you weren't due back for a couple of days?' he said to Saoirse.

'I wasn't. But it seems I have a job interview in a couple of days, so we came home early.' She walked over to him and hugged him. 'Are you OK?'

'Yes.' The lie was automatic. He glanced at Izzy. Did she know about the baby? Did Saoirse? Did they know Vittoria had come to London today, so that was the real reason why they'd come back early?

Probably not, he thought, or one of them would've said something by now.

This was a mess. Fighting with Vittoria wasn't making either of them happy, and it would hurt their sisters, too.

He didn't even know where to start unpicking this and making it right. Maybe he needed to sleep on it.

'So, what's this interview?' he asked.

'It's at the V&A—in the department where I worked on that exhibition.'

She'd loved that, he remembered. To the point where she'd added more textile modules into her degree. 'And the interview's in a couple of days? They're not giving you much notice.'

'The notification was in my spam box,' she said. 'Luckily I had to check something else and found it. So I'm home early to give me some time to do the prep.'

'Well, it's good to have you home. I missed you.' And he meant it. Though he was glad she hadn't been there when he'd come back from that meeting with Vittoria, feeling bruised and rejected and utterly miserable. 'When do you plan to go back to San Rocello, Izzy? Or are you staying in London for a bit?' It was like picking at a scab, and he only just stopped himself asking her when she'd last seen her sister or when she was going to see her again. Whether she could maybe make Vittoria see sense…

'I'm staying in London for a bit,' she said. 'While I was away, I was offered an internship with a design agency.'

'And your family's OK about it?'

She nodded. 'I talked to Rina about it. Being her, she asked me all kinds of awkward questions—to make sure I was doing the right thing for me. She's scary when she's in Winter Queen mode.'

Something like he'd seen today. 'Uh-huh,' he said.

'She doesn't mean it when she's being all cold.'

Didn't she? 'How do you know?' The question came out before he could stop it.

'When I was younger, sometimes I thought she was freezing me out—and later I realised she was doing it to protect me,' Izzy explained. 'There was this one time, when I was fifteen, and I desperately wanted her to take me to this party because I knew this guy in her set, a guy I really fancied, was going. She flatly refused and went all Winter Queen on me. Every time I knew he was going to be somewhere she was going, I asked her to take me. She always refused and froze me out when I tried to discuss it with her. I resented it for months. But about a year later I heard a rumour about him. It seemed he wasn't very good at understanding the word no. Rina knew I liked him, but she also knew I was too young to listen to her warning me off him—that I'd probably think I could change him—so instead she froze me out. She refused to take me to any social events with her, so I wouldn't be anywhere near him and risk being alone with him. She did it to protect me.'

Freezing Izzy to protect her...

Vittoria had frozen him, this afternoon. Completely.

And that still hurt. He turned the subject back to art, until Izzy left for her own flat and Saoirse had gone to run herself a bath.

And then, when he was alone, he let himself think about it.

Vittoria had frozen him out after he'd sent the bluebell picture.

Was there something about bluebells that might have upset her?

He couldn't think of anything. So what, then? Had she not known how to reply?

He couldn't work it out.

But he did know she'd planned to talk to her family about the arranged marriage. And there was the fact that she was pregnant. Did any of her family know about the baby? Or was he the first person she'd told?

He thought about it some more. Was she freezing him out to protect him, the way she'd frozen out Izzy to protect her? Did she have to marry the Spanish duke's son, after all?

No. That didn't feel right.

He was missing something—like when you cropped a photograph in the wrong place. What was in the gap?

He flicked through the photographs in his private portfolio and found the one of Vittoria in the library: the bookworm, the woman who lit up around words. Another of her at the beach, when she'd been looking for fossils and beachcombing without a care in the world. Another, in the bluebell wood.

And then there was the portrait that was only in his head: the woman who'd woken in his arms.

All of those pictures were warm.

None of them—not even the formal ones he'd taken for the palace—was like the woman he'd faced today. The scary Winter Queen.

Had today been an act?

He'd taken her words at face value, and he'd been hurt and angry. But had he misunderstood?

He thought about it.

Vittoria was facing a dilemma that countless women had faced before her: an unplanned pregnancy. It was the twenty-first century and attitudes towards single parenthood had changed—unless you were a royal. The new queen being a single mum would cause a massive scandal in San Rocello.

What choices did she have?

The obvious one was a termination. But she'd made it clear that she planned to keep the baby.

And she wouldn't step down from taking over from her grandfather, because she'd spent years in training to be queen. And Liam knew she felt the same way about her little sister as he did about his: a fierce, protective love. She'd never just dump her responsibilities on her little sister and expect Izzy to take over as the queen. Apart from the fact that Izzy had never had the training, Izzy wanted a career in art. Vittoria would support her.

She'd love the baby, too. Her 'resources' weren't just financial. Of course she'd want her child to have a different upbringing from her own—one where the baby felt loved and valued for him or herself, not just because this child was next in line to the throne.

And she'd been well aware that if Liam was her partner, he'd have to give up his career and the life he'd worked so hard to make for himself. So had she pushed him away so he didn't have to choose between the career he wanted and the family he'd said he didn't want? Had she given him what she thought he wanted— what he'd told her he wanted?

But now he realised that wasn't what he wanted. At all.

He wanted her. He wanted their baby. He wanted to make a family with her.

And he needed to tell her.

The only thing was, if he phoned her he had the strongest feeling she'd let his call go to voicemail and push him to talk to her solely through their lawyers.

Izzy had been her normal self with him today, which he didn't think would be the case if she knew about the baby and what a mess he'd made of seeing her sister today. It wasn't his place to break the news to her, so he couldn't ask for her help in setting up a meeting with Vittoria.

But there was one person who might be able to help.

He grabbed his phone and dialled the number.

'Mr MacCarthy?'

'Yes. Mr...' Liam realised then that he didn't actually know Giorgio's surname. 'Giorgio. I'm so sorry to disturb you, but I need your help.'

'Really?' Giorgio drawled. 'I don't think there's anything I can do to help you.'

'Please don't hang up,' Liam said swiftly. 'Please just give me three minutes of your time. I know you're close to the princess and you told me you think of her as your little sister—and right now you probably want to punch me.'

'There is that,' Giorgio agreed, his voice very cool.

'I've been an idiot. I'm assuming you know the full situation?'

Giorgio was silent. Which told Liam nothing.

OK. He'd try to do this without mentioning the baby, then, just in case Vittoria's bodyguard didn't know. 'I'm firmly in the wrong,' he said. 'I should have dug deeper and been more honest—with myself as well as with

Her Royal Highness.' He took a deep breath. 'I need to talk to her. Face to face, and in private—well, obviously if she wants you there then I'd be guided by her wishes.'

'Then why don't you call her?'

'Because I pushed her too far this morning and I don't think she'll answer my call. I think she expects my lawyer to be in touch with hers.'

'Then I don't see how I can help.'

'You care about her,' Liam said. 'And you knew this Rufus guy.'

'Yes.'

'I'm not Rufus. I nearly let her down the way he did—but I've realised now I was listening to the words coming out of her mouth instead of what she was really saying.'

'Why are you asking me to help and not Princess Isabella?' Giorgio asked.

'Because I don't know how much Izzy knows—actually, I don't know how much *you* know,' Liam admitted. 'I don't want to make things difficult between Izzy and my sister. I'm trying to find a way that causes least hurt to everyone.'

'That's fair.'

'So can you help me, please? If I get on the first plane tomorrow to San Rocello, could you persuade the princess to meet me? Say, twenty minutes?'

'Twenty minutes is a long time.'

'If I haven't fixed things by then, you can punch me. Hard as you like,' Liam said.

There was the ghost of a smile in Giorgio's voice as he said, 'I rather think the princess can do that for herself.'

'She probably could,' Liam said dryly. 'She wouldn't need to do it physically.'

'All right. Come to the palace, and I'll tell Matteo Battaglia to expect you. Let me know your arrival time.'

'Thank you, Giorgio. I really appreciate it.'

'Don't hurt her again,' Giorgio said.

'I won't. Just so you know, I hurt her through stupidity, not because I meant to,' Liam said. 'I'd never hurt her intentionally.' He paused. 'One more thing. Can the meeting be in her father's rose garden?'

'That,' Giorgio said, 'convinces me more than anything else you've said.'

'Thank you,' Liam said. 'I won't let her down again.'

The second he ended the call, he went online to book the first possible flight to San Rocello. To his relief, there was one seat left on an early flight in the morning. He booked it and texted the details to Giorgio.

The following morning, Liam felt ridiculously nervous. This was the most important meeting of his life. If he got it wrong…

But his shoes were clean, his shirt was pressed and his tie was tied properly. Just what he could remember his mum telling him to do on what he'd once thought was the most important meeting of his life, his interview at Edinburgh university.

'Wish me luck now, Mum,' he whispered. 'Because I really, really need it.'

He propped a note for Saoirse against the kettle, to tell her he was out all day at a meeting, then drove to the airport.

Having no luggage and the minimum carry-on meant that check-in and security clearance were swift. Giorgio had sent him a text confirming that the meeting was set up in the rose garden. Liam settled into his seat on the aeroplane and tried to put himself into Vittoria's shoes. Was she as mixed up over this as he was? Hurt, angry, afraid?

But he couldn't second-guess her. All he could do was be honest with her. Listen to her—and listen properly, this time. Tell her how he really felt.

She was the queen-to-be. Fair, impartial, believing in justice. So he knew she'd listen to him. He just hoped she wanted the same thing he did.

Although everything ran on time, the journey seemed to take for ever—plane, ferry, taxi—but at last he was outside the palace. The last time he'd gone through the palace security measures it had been to take some photographs, which were an important move in his career. This time, the stakes were so much higher.

The Private Secretary took him through to the palace gardens, where Giorgio was waiting.

'Thank you for arranging this, Giorgio,' Liam said.

'Don't let her down,' was all the bodyguard said, and took him through to the rose garden.

Vittoria was sitting on a wrought iron seat under a bower of roses, reading. Every bit of her exuded calm; but when Liam was close enough to see her eyes, he could tell that she was as nervous about this as he was.

'Thank you for agreeing to see me,' he said.

She inclined her head in acknowledgement.

Giorgio said something in rapid Italian which Liam couldn't follow, then walked over to the end of the garden. They were still in his line of sight, but had the privacy to speak frankly.

'First off,' Liam said, 'I apologise. I was an idiot. I was listening to what was coming out of your mouth instead of listening to what you were really saying.'

'Uh-huh.' She wasn't giving a millimetre;

right now, Liam knew that he was talking to the Winter Queen.

How was he going to get through to her?

'Secondly,' he said, 'are you all right?'

'I'm fine,' she said. 'Why did you come here today?'

To tell you I love you and I want to make a family with you.

But if he told her that, he had a feeling she'd throw it back in his face. She was still being formal with him, and he needed her to feel comfortable enough to open up to him again. So he'd make the concessions.

'To listen,' he said instead. 'To understand.'

Her eyes narrowed. 'We said it all yesterday. There's nothing else to listen to and nothing else to understand. I'm pregnant and you're fighting me for custody.'

'Let's rewind a bit,' he said. 'I think the conversation we had yesterday went very, very wrong for both of us. So let's go back a couple of weeks.'

She frowned. 'A couple of weeks?'

'Yes.' To something he hadn't quite understood at the time, but he'd done some research since. 'You and Izzy called it your *Roman Holiday,*' he said, 'so I'm assuming you know the film?'

She looked surprised, but nodded.

'I didn't—so I looked it up. And it wasn't a *Roman Holiday*,' he said quietly. 'Yes, on a superficial level, there are similarities. The princess in the film spends time as a commoner, and so did you. But that's as far as it goes. This isn't the nineteen-fifties, and Giorgio was with us when we went to the cottage by the sea. I never had any intention of writing a story about you for the press. I didn't have a fight with anyone, you didn't rescue me from a river, and I didn't bring you back to San Rocello.'

She said nothing.

'The kiss happened.' He paused. 'In the film, they don't spend the night together. But we did.' He took a deep breath. 'I woke with you in my arms. It was perfect.'

She said nothing, but at least she wasn't disagreeing. And the faint colour in her cheeks gave him hope.

'And, that night, we made a baby.'

'But you gave me all the photos from my time with you. Just like in the film.'

'No, I gave you *access* to them,' he corrected. 'I still have the originals—and maybe one day I might publish them.' Before the look of horror in her eyes bloomed any further, he said swiftly, 'Though, if I do, firstly it will only be with your full permission, and secondly you get to choose which ones we publish. And, going back to the film, there's another really important difference. I'm the photographer, not the journalist.' He waited until she met his gaze, before finishing quietly, 'I'm not the one who walks away.'

'You said you didn't want to raise a family,' she reminded him, 'because you've already done that with Saoirse. You said you wanted to concentrate on your career.'

'I know what I told you, and it's exactly how I thought I felt,' he said. 'But you're expecting our baby, and that changes everything.'

For a moment she wasn't the Winter Queen any more; she was the woman whose smile was like sunshine. Even though her mouth wasn't smiling, her eyes were. Just enough to give him hope.

'But, just so we're clear, I'm not here because of the baby.'

Her face shuttered. 'You said you'd stand by me. Do the right thing.'

'You'd only just told me you were pregnant,' he said, 'and I wasn't thinking straight. It was a knee-jerk reaction. And then you told me I didn't need to be involved—so I think we hurt each other. But I'm sorry I hurt you.'

'I'm sorry, too,' she said.

'I'm not going to fight you for custody. I don't want to hurt you. Ever. I should have told you how much I missed you, when you left to come back to San Rocello. That's why I sent you the picture of a rose.'

'A picture's worth a thousand words—but I didn't really know what you were trying to tell me.'

'I think most people have the same idea what a single red rose means,' he said dryly. 'But it wasn't just that. It was all the other stuff that goes with a rose for me. Your favourite poem. Our conversation, that last morning. What you told me about missing your dad. It's why I wanted to meet you here—in a place that I know has happy memories for you, a place that means *family* to you.' He looked at her. 'And you sent me a photo of a seashell. What did that mean?'

'I picked it up on the beach. I wanted you to think about the beach, where you kissed me for the first time.' She looked straight at him. 'And where we walked together, the day we made the baby.'

Was she telling him she loved him?

He still wasn't sure.

But those memories made him feel warm all over.

'And then you sent me a photo of a bluebell,' she said.

'Because it was the colour of your eyes,'

he said. 'And the carpet of the woods where I taught you how to take a good portrait.' He looked at her. 'Did you look up its meaning?'

'No.'

'You should have done,' he said softly. But that was where their flirting by photographs had ended.

'What does it mean?' she asked.

'Everlasting love. Constancy,' he said, and waited for that to sink in. 'And then,' he said, 'you ghosted me. Did you change your mind about me?'

She shook her head. 'I didn't know what to say. I remembered you saying you thought my eyes were the same colour as bluebells, so I was going to send you a cornflower—that's the colour of *your* eyes. But then I looked up the meaning of a cornflower. Apparently, it's "delicacy and refinement". And that wasn't what I wanted to say.'

He laughed. 'I'm not delicate—or that refined. But you are.'

She shrugged. 'I didn't know what to say to you,' she said. 'I didn't know if you were just flirting with me or if you were serious. And then I had something to sort out for Nonno. And time just got away from me, and the longer it went on the harder it was to know what to say to you. In business, I know what I'm doing.

When it comes to emotional stuff, I'm not so sure of myself. The last time I was in love, I thought Rufus loved me all the way back. But he didn't. He walked away.'

'I know,' Liam said softly. 'But I'm not Rufus, and I'm not walking away.'

'But you said you want to concentrate on your career.'

'I do,' he said. 'But I also want a family. I know I told you I didn't—at the time, I *thought* I didn't. But this baby has made me think about what I really want.' He paused. 'Izzy said you used to freeze her out to protect her. And I think that's what you did to me yesterday; you pushed me away, because you didn't want me to feel I had to choose between you and doing what I love.'

She stared at him, those beautiful bluebell eyes widening slightly.

'But the thing is,' he said, 'that's not quite what I want any more.' He paused. 'Ask me what I want, Vittoria.'

Her voice was cool, calm and collected, as was her expression; but he could see by the shallowness of her breathing that she felt anything but cool and calm and collected. 'What do you want, Liam?'

The fact she'd used his first name gave him hope.

'I want *you*,' he said softly. 'I want to be a family with you and our baby. Not because I feel it's my duty but because I want to be with you. Both of you. And not because you're a princess, because I couldn't care less about how much money you're worth or how far back you can trace your family tree. Titles, diamonds, castles—none of it matters. The important thing is love.'

Her eyes glittered with unshed tears. 'Are you saying that you love me?'

'Yes, I love you, Vittoria,' he said. 'And I want to marry you. I want to make a life with you. I want to wake up with you every morning and I want to go to sleep at night with you beside me. I want to teach our baby—our children, if we're lucky—how to build sandcastles. I want to teach them to count and to read and to grow roses and to take photographs. But I don't want just the fun parenting stuff. I want to be there when they wake in the night and need a cuddle, or when they're out of sorts and need someone to listen—whether they're tiny or a stroppy teen, or in years to come maybe when they're an adult with their own children. And I want to do it all with you. Because I love you.'

She swallowed hard. 'You mean that?'

'Yes. And I want you to be sure that I love you for yourself, Vittoria. As far as your family is concerned, I'm from the wrong background—I'm not the son of a royal. But I grew up knowing I was loved, and I brought up my little sister so she was secure and knew she was loved. I believe that's worth more than all the money and castles and power in the world.' His throat felt thick, but until she believed him, he was going to keep talking. 'The only thing that matters is love. I'll tell that to your grandparents and your mother. And I'll keep on telling them until they understand that I love you for your own sake, and that I'm prepared to learn whatever you need me to so I can support you and be your anchor when you become queen.'

'You love me.' Her voice was full of wonder.

'I love you,' he confirmed.

'You really, really love me.'

He coughed. 'This is where you're supposed to say it back. But only if you mean it.'

'I love you,' she said. 'And I mean that.' She took a deep breath. 'But is that enough?'

'It is for me. Isn't it enough for you?' he asked.

'Of course it is. But I come with complications. And it means you have to give things up. I don't want you to do that. You've worked so hard. I can't ask you to give up your career.'

'I won't be giving up my career,' he said. 'Mine's a little more flexible than yours. I'm at the stage where I can choose which jobs I accept. I put my career on hold for my sister, because I love her—and I'll put it on hold again whenever I need to for our baby. And for *you*.'

A tear rolled down her cheek, and he risked leaning over and wiping it away with the pad of his thumb.

'Don't cry. It's going to be fine. I love you, I'm here, and I'm not going anywhere. Well, I do have to go somewhere, just for a little while,' he corrected himself. 'Saoirse has an interview tomorrow. I want to be there to make her breakfast, calm her last-minute nerves and remind her that she knows her stuff, to just be herself in front of the interviewer and remember to breathe. I'm her only family, and I won't abandon her. But I'll always be there for you, too.'

Vittoria remembered him talking about the girlfriends who'd wanted him to put them first and ignore his little sister's needs. 'If she's got an interview, I'd expect you to be there—just as I'd want to support my own sister,' she said. 'I'll never try to make you feel guilty or tear you in two.'

'Thank you.'

'But,' she warned, 'being with me—it's not going to be easy. Being a royal means everyone watches you, every minute of every day, and judges you. You can't ever be grouchy or look tired, because people will speculate and spin stories. It's like living in a goldfish bowl. Rufus walked away rather than dealing with it.'

He looked grim. 'I'm making a supposition here, but I'm guessing that's one of the reasons why your mother wants you to marry someone who was born into it—someone who's been brought up coping with it and won't let you down.'

'It is,' she agreed.

'I'm not Rufus. And we need to learn how to manage the press,' he said. 'We'll make friends with them. Work with them. Instead of trying to be perfect, we will show them the human side of the palace. That you're like every other mum-to-be who has morning sickness. That I'm like every other dad who's grouchy after a broken night when I'm trying to hit a deadline. We'll let the press share our family, and then they'll protect us.'

She thought about it. 'Share our family.'

He nodded. 'Though this is all a bit of a moot point, because you haven't agreed to marry me yet.'

'You haven't actually asked me,' she pointed out.

'I will,' he said. 'And I also want to talk to your family.'

'You mean ask their permission?'

'Not so much permission,' he said, 'because you're not anyone's property, but I'd like their blessing. I want to be courteous and show them that I'm considering their feelings, too. I don't have a royal background, but they need to know that I'll love you and cherish you for the rest of my days—and I intend to stay right by your side, whatever happens.'

She could barely believe that he loved her and wanted to be by her side. Be a hands-on dad.

'I don't have a ring in my pocket, and I think Saoirse should have our mum's engagement ring, so I can't offer you that in the future, either.' He smiled. 'So I guess we're going to have to go shopping at some point.' He dropped to one knee. 'I kind of wanted to ask you in the palace library, where it all started. But then I saw you reading on this bench, and I know that this is the right place. I hope your dad's looking down right now and knows I'm asking you to marry me in the place that he loved most. I hope my dad's there with him, swapping plant stories. And my mum's making them both a mug of tea so they can skulk off into a greenhouse afterwards and potter about and talk about which parks are the best for taking toddlers to.'

She felt the tears filling her eyes. 'That's—that's a lovely picture.'

'And I have weddingy demands.'

She couldn't help smiling. 'Weddingy demands?'

'Absolutely. I want this to be a family wedding. Izzy and Sursh as our bridesmaids. Your grandfather walking you down the aisle. Your mum and your grandmother dabbing their eyes in the front row and sighing over what a fairy tale bride you make.'

'Works for me,' she said.

'Good.' He smiled up at her. 'Vittoria di Sarda, I fell in love with you on the day I first met you,' he said. 'And even when you had the wrong colour hair and the wrong colour eyes, and you were wearing clothes you wouldn't normally wear in a million years, I fell deeper in love with you every day. I'm not promising you perfection—there will be days when I'm grouchy with you and you're the Winter Queen with me, and you're going to criticise or choke on my coffee—but I promise to love you with all of my heart, all of my soul, all that I am. If your family gives us their blessing, will you marry me?'

'Yes,' she said, and kissed him.

CHAPTER TEN

'So, DO I ask Matteo Battaglia to make me an appointment with your grandfather?' Liam asked.

'No. We're doing this as a team,' Vittoria said.

'If you come with me, it looks as if I'm hiding behind your skirts,' Liam pointed out. 'If I can't even face your grandfather on my own, how is he ever going to believe that I can cope with a royal lifestyle and a pack of paparazzi?'

She looked at him thoughtfully. 'You have a point. But Matteo can stonewall you and claim that Nonno's diary is full and you'll have to accept what he says at face value; whereas I also have access to Nonno's diary and I know where the gaps are.'

'In that case,' Liam said, 'I'll apologise to your grandfather's private secretary later for going behind his back and ask you to make an appointment for me.' He paused. 'Do you know when your mother and grandmother are free, too?'

'You're planning to face all of them at once?'

'That makes it sound as if it's going to be an ordeal,' Liam said.

She had to be honest. 'It might be.'

He shrugged. 'In the old days, weren't knights supposed to fight dragons to win the princess's hand? This is the modern equivalent.'

She raised an eyebrow. 'Really?'

He laughed. 'Except obviously you're not a chattel to be given away.'

'And there's the whole dragon-slaying thing,' she pointed out.

'All right, it was a stupid metaphor,' he said. 'I was trying to be too clever, and I failed.'

She kissed him lightly. 'I like the fact you can admit when you're wrong.'

'Let's rewind,' he said. 'I'd like to meet your family and ask for their blessing. Obviously, they'll have concerns, so I'd like the chance to talk to them, find out what worries them, and either reassure them or work towards reassuring them. And I know that sounds more like a business deal than planning a wedding,' he added swiftly, 'so I also want you to know that I love you and I'm going to do whatever it takes to make you happy.'

A man who thought things through. Who planned. Who did things sensibly—and who loved her and wasn't afraid to tell her. 'That,' she said, 'sounds like an excellent plan.'

'With goals. Specific, measurable, achievable, realistic—the only thing missing is "timed",' he said, smiling. 'And I think the timing is now. Provided they're free, of course.'

Three brief phone calls later—all conducted in rapid Italian Liam couldn't follow—Vittoria turned to him. 'Would you like to accompany me to the library? They'll meet us there.'

The library.

The place where it had all started. Where he'd seen the woman behind the tiara. The woman he'd fallen in love with.

That had to be a good sign—right?

Vittoria signalled to Giorgio that all was well, and took Liam's hand.

Liam's stomach was tied in knots. This was the most important meeting of his life, and he had to get it right. He needed to convince Vittoria's family that he was the right partner for her—even though he was from the wrong background.

Right at that moment, it felt like every exam, his driving test, and every 'first day' of his life rolled into one. Knowing he needed to prove himself. Except with exams and his career, he'd known what he was doing. He'd been pretty sure of the results, because he'd put the work in and honed the skills he needed.

This was something he had no control over, and it was terrifying.

Silently, he walked beside her.

He only realised he was gripping her hand too tightly when she whispered, 'Liam, I kind of need some circulation in my fingers. Would you mind loosening your grip?'

'Sorry.' He dropped her hand. 'I didn't mean to hurt you.'

'It's fine.' She stole a swift kiss and laced her fingers very loosely between his again. 'It's kind of reassuring to know you're nervous.'

'How?'

'Because it means I'm that important to you,' she said. 'You're not taking any of this for granted.'

'No. But, whatever happens today, I love you and I'll be there for you and the baby. I'll make it work,' he promised.

She paused outside the door to the library. 'Ready?'

Not in a million years. 'Ready,' he confirmed.

'I love you,' she whispered, and stood back to let him open the door for her.

Vittoria's family were sitting on the comfortable sofas arranged in a semi-circle in the centre of the room—the king, the queen and the princess. Although the setting appeared to make it informal, Liam knew it wasn't informal in the slightest. It wasn't normal for a princess to ask the rest of the royal family to a meeting, and it wasn't normal to introduce a commoner at said meeting. Her family were astute enough to realise this was an interview. He was going to be the one doing most of the talking and answering their questions. And the seating was set up very much like an interview panel.

'Nonno, Nonna, Mamma—I'd like to introduce you to Liam MacCarthy,' Vittoria said. 'Liam, you have already met my grandfather, King Vittorio. This is my grandmother, Queen Giulia, and my mother, Princess Maria.'

Liam gave a formal bow. *'Vostro Maestà, Vostre Altezze Reale,'* he said.

Three inscrutable royal faces gazed back at him. And nobody asked him to take a seat. Maybe this was a test to show that he could cope with pressure. Well, he'd make sure he passed—because this was too important to fail. He couldn't and wouldn't let Vittoria down.

'We were very pleased with your official photographs of Vittoria, Mr MacCarthy,' the king said.

'Thank you, sir.' Liam smiled.

'And it was kind of you to host Vittoria in England,' Queen Giulia added.

The politeness oddly made him feel even more nervous. Perhaps it would be better to think of this in terms of an assignment. He needed to get the pose right and the lighting right, and bring out the story behind the picture.

Except in this case he was the subject, and he had no control over the pose or the lighting.

'What brings you to San Rocello, Mr MacCarthy?' Princess Maria asked.

This was it. His moment. Liam glanced at Vittoria, who gave an almost imperceptible nod.

'I was hoping to speak to you all,' Liam said. 'Sir. Ma'am. Ma'am.'

Again, they had inscrutable expressions. No feedback. It was like working in a room with a difficult light source and without a light meter to help him get the balance right; he had to rely on his own instincts. Make sure that he was enough.

'I realise that this might come as a—' Shock? No, because that signalled bad news. For a moment, he wished he'd asked Vittoria to delay the meeting for long enough for him to work out a speech. Then again, even with preparation he might get it wrong. It was better to speak from the heart. Be honest. 'A surprise,' he continued, 'but I would like your blessing to marry Vittoria.'

'You want to marry Vittoria,' the king said. 'Perhaps you could explain why you think we would give you our blessing, Mr MacCarthy.'

'Because I love her, sir,' Liam said. 'I mean I love *Vittoria*—it has nothing to do with her being a princess, and everything to do with who she is.'

'So do we assume from this that you had some kind of affair during Vittoria's holiday?' the queen asked.

He wanted to squirm, but he faced her. 'That,' Liam said, 'makes our relationship sound tacky and flimsy. Which it isn't. With respect, ma'am, I fell in love with your granddaughter the first day I met her.' He took a deep breath. 'When I took photographs for her sister in this very room.'

Silence.

He had no idea whether this was going well or badly. All he could do was press on. 'Obviously I'm not from a royal background, and I realise that might cause you some concern about my suitability. But I'd like to reassure you that I will always put Vittoria first. And that I love her.'

'I see,' Vittorio said. 'And you can support

my granddaughter in the manner to which she has become accustomed?'

'Not quite,' Liam said. 'I'm not a prince. I can't shower her in priceless jewels, buy her a castle in every country, or employ dozens of staff. But I have a comfortable income, I have a good reputation in my industry, and I own a flat in Chelsea as well as the cottage by the sea. I have supported my family for years.' He met the king's gaze levelly. 'I'm aware that I'm not the kind of person you expected Vittoria to marry. I apologise for that, but I'm not ashamed of my background. My father was a horticulturalist at Kew Gardens, and my mother taught art. They were good people, kind and loving, and I hope I can bring that same goodness, kindness and love into our marriage.'

And oh, he dearly wanted what his parents had had. A marriage where they'd worked as a team and backed each other. Loved each other.

Vittoria's mother and grandmother exchanged a glance. Liam was horribly aware that his words were inadequate.

What would he worry about, in their shoes? What had gone wrong with Rufus? Apparently the man had backed away because he couldn't handle the royal lifestyle. So Vittoria's family might worry that he would do the same. 'I know a royal life isn't an easy one, especially as it's lived very much in the public eye, and I'll probably make mistakes,' Liam said. 'But I hope that someone on your staff will point me in the right direction to help me learn whatever I need to know, so I can support Vittoria properly in her duties and not repeat my mistakes. Right now, my Italian's at a very basic level, but I intend to become fluent as quickly as possible. And I'm not afraid of hard work.'

'No. A man who put his own dreams aside to bring up his younger sister definitely isn't afraid of hard work,' Vittorio said.

The king had clearly either seen that dossier Vittoria had read before Liam took her portrait, or she'd briefed him.

'And how do you feel about all this, Vittoria?' the king asked.

'I love Liam,' she said simply. 'And he loves me. That's all I need to know.'

'I see,' he said, and turned to Liam. 'So, Mr MacCarthy. What if I don't give you my blessing to marry my granddaughter?'

Liam lifted his chin slightly and looked at the king. 'Family is important to both of us. With respect, sir, we intend to marry whether we have your blessing or not. But we'd both be happier if we had our family there to share the celebration and the love.'

'Celebration,' the king said thoughtfully. 'Should I assume you want a full state wedding?'

'I want,' Liam said, 'whatever will make Vittoria happy. Whether it's a simple and very private family ceremony, or whether it's a more elaborate celebration so her country can share in it. The type of wedding isn't important. What's important is that we're together. A team. And that our families are there.'

Was it his imagination, or was there a tiny glint of approval in the king's eyes?

OK. So they understood he loved Vittoria, he was prepared to work hard to make sure he fitted in to a royal lifestyle, and he intended to be constant. What else would a rich family be worried about? That he was a gold-digger who planned to steal the princess's heart, then dump her and take her to the cleaners, perhaps? 'I will instruct my family lawyer to arrange a prenup, to say that I am entitled to absolutely nothing if this marriage doesn't last,' Liam added. 'Though I do believe this marriage will last, because I love Vittoria and that's not going to change. Ever. I will love her—' and their baby, though he rather thought that particular piece of news needed to wait for a little bit longer '—with all my heart and soul, for the rest of my days.' He looked at them. 'Is there anything you're concerned about that I haven't addressed?'

'Being a consort isn't easy,' Giulia said. 'How do you propose to cope with that side of Vittoria's life?'

That was an easier question. 'As the queen of your country,' he said, 'Vittoria will have a lot to think about and a lot to worry about. My job as her consort, ma'am, will be to take some of that care from her. To be there when she needs me, but not wrapping her in cotton wool or crowding her. Supporting her. Holding her hand when she thinks the next step she needs to take will be too hard, and reminding her that she's an incredibly capable woman who can do absolutely anything she puts her mind to.'

'Well, young man,' Giulia said. 'It seems you understand what a consort's role is.'

'And I intend to do it well.' Liam took a deep breath. 'Of course you have concerns— just as I would about anyone who wanted to marry my sister. You love Vittoria and you want the best for her. The way I see it, Vittoria needs the support of someone who loves her. Someone who will listen to her worries, let her bounce ideas, ask questions to help clarify her thoughts, and help her to find a solution. She needs someone who will put her first, and that

to me is worth more than any title or money
I could bring to a marriage. I can't offer perfection, but I will love her with all my heart
and soul—all that I am—for the rest of my
days. And I'm prepared to do whatever it takes
to make this work. I know you only have my
word for it, but I hope that Princess Isabella
can reassure you that I'm honourable. That I
have integrity.'

'How do you know you love Vittoria, Mr
MacCarthy?' Maria asked.

'Because my world's a better place with her
in it, ma'am,' Liam said. 'And without her everything feels as if it's monochrome and un-
derexposed. She's the one who brings the light
in, for me.'

'You've known Vittoria for, what, a month?
How do you know your feelings won't change?'
Giulia asked.

Vittoria had told him that her mother and
grandmother were overprotective. But he understood where they were coming from; they
were asking the same kind of questions he'd
want answered by anyone who wanted to
marry Saoirse.

All he could do was speak from the heart.
Tell them how he really felt.

'My feelings probably will change, ma'am,'
he said. 'I love Vittoria for who she is now. But

people aren't static and neither is love. People grow and change. But I think Vittoria and I are both old enough to realise how each other is likely to change in the years to come. And I know I'll love the woman she becomes.' He took a deep breath. 'I can stand here and declare my undying love for the next hour, but they're just words. You have no way of knowing that I mean them, and I can't say anything to prove how I feel about Vittoria. But I think I can show you.'

'How?' the king asked.

'May I show you the photograph I took, sir?' He gestured to his phone.

At the king's nod, Liam tapped in the password to his private portfolio and brought up the last picture he'd taken in the library.

'A good portrait will show you the person behind the image,' he said. 'And, looking back, I think this is the moment I fell in love with Vittoria. This is the woman behind the tiara. She's bright and capable, a little shy, and she loses herself in Shakespeare.'

The king studied the photograph, then handed the phone to the queen. She, too, examined it, then passed it to Vittoria's mother. And Maria gave a sharp intake of breath. 'My daughter,' she said softly. 'I've never seen you like that, Rina. You glow.'

'That's the woman I see,' Liam said, his voice equally soft. 'The woman I want to spend the rest of my days with. The woman I want to grow old with. The woman I want to have ch—' He stopped.

'Go on, Mr MacCarthy,' the queen said.

Liam glanced at Vittoria. Should this come from him or from her?

Or perhaps from both of them. He'd said they were a team. Now was their first chance to prove it.

'There is one more thing we need to tell you about,' he said quietly, and took her hand.

This was the turning point, Vittoria knew. The moment where her family would accept or reject Liam. And it was so, so important that they accepted him.

'One little thing,' Vittoria said. 'Nonno, Nonna, Mamma—or perhaps I should say Bisnonno, Bisnonna and Nonna.'

Just as she'd expected, her grandparents and her mother looked at her in utter shock.

'You're pregnant?' Maria asked finally. 'How pregnant?'

'It's very early days,' Vittoria said. 'I did the test a few days ago. I know Liam and I have done this completely the wrong way round—traditionally it should be marriage, then a coronation, and then a christening. I know we're disappointing you, and I'm sorry about that.'

'Is that why you want to marry my granddaughter, Mr MacCarthy?' the king asked. 'Because of the baby?'

'No. I want to marry your granddaughter because I love her,' Liam repeated. 'And, even though the baby isn't planned, he or she will be very much loved. I'm prepared to do my share of changing nappies and getting up in the night.' His voice thickened slightly as he said, 'I hope our baby will grow up with a grandmother and great-grandparents who love him or her as much as I know my parents would have loved a grandchild.'

Vittoria knew that was going to be hard for him, not being able to share his baby with his parents. Just as it would be for her, only being able to share memories and photographs of her father, rather than seeing him give her child a piggyback through his beloved rose garden. 'And my father,' she added softly.

'Francesco.' Maria blinked back tears. 'Your father loved babies, Rina. Yes, you're right. He would have loved being a Nonno. And I...' She shook her head. 'This wasn't what I expected to hear today.'

'I'm sorry I've disappointed you, Mamma,'

Vittoria said. 'I know this isn't what you and Nonna wanted for me.'

'Maybe,' Maria said, 'we were wrong. Maybe love is more important than a shared background.' She looked at Liam. 'It's not going to be easy, but you seem to have both feet on the ground, Mr MacCarthy. Being practical and pragmatic... Those are important qualities in this world.'

'Love is the most important thing,' Liam said. 'It's easy for me to talk. But please don't judge me now, ma'am. I'd like you all to judge me in a year's time—when you'll have seen me prove my words every day. When you've seen me change nappies, bring Vittoria co—no, not coffee, because Izzy says my coffee's terrible, a cup of tea,' he corrected, making Vittoria smile. 'When you've seen me settle a teething baby, when you've seen me noticing that little pleat between her eyes that Vittoria has when she worries about something and I've persuaded her to talk to me so I can share her worries and reassure her. When you've seen me be there.'

'A year's time. When we'll have a baby's laughter in the palace again,' Giulia said. 'And, a year after that, pattering feet. It will be nice to have a child in the garden again.'

'A wedding, a christening and a coronation,' the king said. He paused, and Vittoria felt the weight of every second. Would her grandfather understand how much she loved Liam? Would her family welcome him? Or was this going to end up rocking the monarchy to its foundations, maybe fracturing it beyond repair?

'Nonno, I hope you won't make me choose between love and duty. I want both,' Vittoria said. 'Liam completes me. With him, I can be myself. I know it's OK to be vulnerable and I know it's OK to lean on him. I trust him. I want to share my life with him. I want our children to grow up, secure that they're loved for themselves.'

The king said nothing, and this time Vittoria couldn't read his eyes. He was totally inscrutable.

'I will do whatever it takes to make this work,' Liam said. 'But the one thing I will not compromise on is my family. I love Vittoria, and I intend to support her. I'll learn whatever I need to. But the one thing I can do well is negotiate with the press. If we make friends with them, if we give them stories, they won't look for faults or gossip. They'll see a queen who understands her people because she shares the same worries that they do, and they'll celebrate her. A bride who worries that she'll trip on the carpet down the aisle, a mum who juggles a busy job with a baby who wakes at three in the morning, a woman who steps up to the top job and wants to do it well so she can lead by example and encourage others to be the best they can be. She isn't Rapunzel in her ivory tower or Sleeping Beauty waiting to be woken. Vittoria's part of the modern world, leading her country and making a difference.'

That was how he saw her? Vittoria wondered. It was a lot to live up to. Daunting.

Until she looked into Liam's eyes and saw the love shining out at her. And that gave her the confidence to believe she really was the woman he saw.

'Vittoria,' Liam finished, 'will be the best queen ever. And I'll be with her, every step of the way.'

And finally, the king smiled. 'All right. You have my blessing, Mr MacCarthy. Liam.'

'Thank you, sir.'

'I think,' the king said, 'in the circumstances you'd better start calling me Nonno.' He rose to his feet, hugged Vittoria, and then shook Liam's hand. 'Congratulations. And welcome to our family.'

Vittoria's mother and grandmother hugged them both.

'And now,' Vittoria's mother said with a smile, 'we have a wedding and a christening to plan…'

EPILOGUE

A year later

'So how do I look?' Vittoria asked, standing in the doorway.

Liam looked at his wife and his heart skipped a beat. 'Breathtaking,' he said. He leant in to whisper in her ear, 'If it wasn't for the fact that your schedule's timed down practically to the second, I'd take you to our room and show you just how gorgeous you look.'

She grinned. 'Later. But I wasn't asking as your wife. How do I look in queenly terms?'

'Perfect,' Maria said, and deftly scooped the baby from Liam's arms. 'Francesca, come to Nonna. Your *babbo* has to get his camera out and take your *mamma's* official coronation photographs.' She kissed the baby, who gurgled and pulled her hair. 'Your father would be so proud of you, Vittoria. As am I.'

'She's beautiful, brave and clever. I think I'm beyond proud,' Liam said.

'Oh, you two.' But Vittoria was laughing.

They'd laughed a lot, this past year. At their wedding, when Liam had scooped her up and danced with her in the palace rose garden. On their honeymoon, when they'd escaped to Liam's little cottage by the sea and walked at the edge of the sea at sunset, kissing as the first stars came out—except, the second week, it turned out that the rest of the San Rocello royal family had rented a stately home nearby and insisted on joining in the celebrations. He'd taken a lot of photographs of the royal family since the day they'd accepted him as Vittoria's husband-to-be, but the ones he took that week were his favourites.

They'd laughed—and cried—when their daughter was born, and agreed that she should be called after both their fathers, Francesca Philippa. The good wishes sent by the people of San Rocello had been humbling in the extreme. Francesca's christening had been a day of national celebration.

And now it was Vittoria's coronation day.

His beautiful queen.

It would be a solemn occasion. But Liam intended it to be full of joy. And, later that night, he was going to enjoy taking off her crown and her gown and making love to the Queen of San Rocello for the very first time.

'What are you thinking?' Vittoria asked.

He grinned. 'Not in front of your mother.'

'She's busy singing to Francesca. She won't hear.'

He leaned over and whispered his thoughts in her ear, and his grin broadened when she blushed.

'That's my queen,' he said. 'I love you, Vittoria. *Ti amo. Per sempre.*'

* * * * *

*If you enjoyed this story,
check out these other great reads from
Kate Hardy*

A Will, a Wish, a Wedding
One Night to Remember
Soldier Prince's Secret Baby Gift
Finding Mr. Right in Florence

All available now!